The First Night

Draco Aleksander

ISBN-10: 1542529808
ISBN-13: 978-1542529808

The First Night

The First Night

I

The young goblin woman's proud saunter became a frenzied run as her home exploded behind her. The large opening of the mine and the guard holes above it glowed and belched smoke as fire ravaged the shaft within. From afar, the entrance took on the appearance of an angry, dying visage, eyes and mouth glowing in the night. Though she had long since been resolved to leave, the circumstances that finally led to it had come abruptly, leaving her with no plan, no supplies, and no time to waste. She raced headlong through the swamp, a streak of yellow-green and reds, as any remaining confidence she had melted away in the intense heat.

Loamy soil squelched beneath her bare feet, and her long coquelicot hair intertwined with the sheer scarlet silk she had clad herself in as she made her escape. The forest behind her glowed with a violent light as the mines beneath it continued to bellow ash and fire. As the destruction spread below, the thinning atmosphere caused the caves which had provided her clan's home and income to collapse and implode, trapping those still within and shaking the very ground for miles around. The black smoke of wet lumber soon filled the air as the flames spread, and the crackling sound of embers

floating on deadly updrafts snapped in the the gobliness'
bat-like ears.

Completely unprotected, save for the nearly
see-through red material, the little lady continued to run, even
as she choked on the noxious air. Fatigue blazed in her lungs,
but adrenaline thrust her into the unknown world, further from
the hell that had once been her home with every step. She had
never even been allowed to walk above ground before, much
less through the forest. Thus, despite growing up beneath the
very soil on which she trod, she relied on blind luck to lead her
out.

Dense trees would have told her that she had not
followed the actual path out of the woods if she had had the
time to stop and think about such things. A taller, more worldly
person would have quickly reached that conclusion after being
lashed by the low, overgrown, and gnarled branches. For the
goblin woman, however, every direction had appeared full of
similar obstacles as the fire threatened to spread. Knotted roots
and thick undergrowth had been between herself and freedom,
so she hastily picked a direction and struck out. She tripped
and recovered every few steps, the momentum of her stride
helping to keep her upright. Occasional snags and jabs from

the foliage went unnoticed as she fixed her eyes on a small patch of blue sky ahead of her.

Without warning, the tree line broke, the ground sloped up dramatically, and the dirt underfoot became significantly more firm. The woman careened forward, the long flow of red fabric swirling around her pale green body as she tumbled up the short, steep slope of the ditch wall that held back the marsh, and landed on the dry packed earth of an unpaved road. She lay there for some time, sobbing softly. Terrified, she knew in her heart that they would come for her.

No one did.

II

The sun wheeled by overhead, afternoon turned to evening, and still the swamp burned. Its smoke blotted out the stars overhead, orange light from below dancing on the black clouds. The dense forest muffled any remaining sounds of civilization that might have been fighting the blaze, and it had become clear to the young gobliness that there was nobody pursuing her.

Getting to her feet, she teetered as she wrapped the delicate material more tightly around herself. It provided almost no protection against the cold of night, but the feeling of having any kind of covering on her body was liberating in a way. She tried to control her breathing, and coughed so hard that she fell back down onto the her knees. Shaking from anxiety and fear, she wretched. Nothing but bile came up, leaving an acrid taste in her mouth.

The small woman stood again, her breathing more stable, and tried to gather her thoughts. Her hair had been fluffed into an unmanageable mane by the chaotic flight, and several attempts to disentangle a number of twigs failed miserably. Looking down, she inspected her mud and grime covered feet. Though they hurt badly, she could not find any serious wounds, and could flex all of her toes without too much pain. She took a deep breath and fixed her dark eyes on the road before her, and began to walk.

More dust gathered on her as she walked, another new experience for the young gobliness. The stone tunnels she was used to were smooth affairs, worn down by generations of people moving about their subterranean world. Even the roughest surfaces of a newly cut branches she had occasionally snuck into were solid and made sense to her. The world aboveground, however, seemed to be made almost entirely of dirt, and the realization that she was becoming slowly coated in it made her skin crawl.

As she continued along the road, however, the glow of the mines faded behind her, giving way to the light of the moon and stars. Her gaze followed the horizon and traveled upwards, and her mouth dropped open as she marveled at the spectacle of the heavens. She had never been able to view it so clearly. Her heart beat faster as all of creation unfolded before her, and tears welled in her eyes once more. She had never realized how beautiful the open sky would be.

The night air gave the gobliness goosebumps, but she felt suddenly alive, and drank in the world around her. The trumpeting of frogs in the ditches mixed with the drumming of crickets in the underbrush, creating a chorus of life that thrummed hypnotically in her ears. She rubbed at her brow, sure that the lightning bugs illuminating the evening were figments of her imagination. Even the strong wind that tried to steal away the fabric in which she had swaddled herself was a breath of fresh air to the young woman on her first evening of freedom.

When another fire loomed at the edge of the road in the distance, she hesitated for a moment out of fear. While this blaze was under control, shadows moved near it, and flickering shapes in the background suggested looming wooden structures on wheels. She remembered seeing something like them near the entrance to the mines once when she had snuck close enough to see her father do business. They had been loading up blocks of the salt that provided her clan's primary income. These wagons, however, seemed much more festive. Even with the ominous shadows of the small fire dancing upon them, their bright and cheerful paint set them apart from the dull work things she had glimpsed.

Ducking into the ditch on the other side of the road, she approached the camp carefully. Frogs croaked and bounced out of the way as the slightly larger green creature passed through their homes. Up to her waist in standing water that would have been only knee-deep to a human, the gobliness was chilled to the bone, and the strip of sheer silk that covered her body was useless against its onslaught. The fire's promise of warmth became more inviting, even though it was tended by strangers. Head just poking over the edge of the roadside, she watched them for a few minutes to try and ascertain their disposition.

"...so if we head to Mirfield, we should be able to both pick up supplies and make a pretty penny if things go our way," said a man in multicolored trousers and a white shirt, half-turned away from her.

"I'm not disagreeing with you," said another, much larger man mostly obscured by the fire and the shadows, "but if we do both, we may not be able to move fast enough to-"

"To what?" said the first man, cutting the second off abruptly, "To make our next destination in time?"

"What? No, I mean…" the larger man began, then trailed off at some unseen signal, "Oh. Of course. We wouldn't get to Briar Glen in time for the...festival."

"Festival?" said another voice. A sandy-haired woman wearing more clothes than the gobliness had ever seen on a female stepped out of one of the wooden structures carrying a shallow metal basin full of meat. Its enticing aroma reached the little lady, even at a distance, and she crept a little higher instinctively.

"Since when is there a festival at this time of year in…" The woman's voice, too, trailed off, and she looked toward the ditch. The gobliness ducked below the edge of the road, realizing that she had long since been seen, and chastising herself for not realizing it sooner.

She had already begun to crawl away when the light of the fire was blotted out by the shape of the larger man. More than three times her height, he grabbed the gobliness by the trailing tail of material in her wake, and easily lifted the minute green woman into the air. She kicked and screamed, baring the shark-like teeth often associated with her race, but gave up as exhaustion met acceptance of her fate.

"Well, she's a weird one," the large man said, his voice booming at an uncomfortable volume up close. His shaved head reflected the fire light off of its back, and his clothes seemed oversized, even on his large body. "Don't think I've ever seen a gobbo' scout like this." As he stepped into the light, she was revealed in greater detail.

"I'd be surprised if you had, Lebar," said the man in multicolored trousers, his smirk audible, "Have you ever seen a 'she' goblin in any case?"

Though she had at first appeared merely pudgy, it became clear that the mass of tangled and mud-soaked fabric hid very feminine features in greater quantities than one would expect on someone of such small stature. Her full lips pouted at the thought of capture, and freckles dotted her cheeks beneath gold-speckled mulberry eyes, which sparkled with reflections of the fire.

"Oh! Oh, I guess you're right…" Lebar said, carrying her unceremoniously, still held at arm's length, "Where did you come from, then?"

The human woman came forward, removing her shawl.

"The poor thing isn't wearing hardly anything," she said, giving the two men disproving looks, "Give her here, now." She took the gobliness, wrapped her in the removed garment, and brought her into the warm circle that pushed back against the night. When placed near the fire, the smaller woman wriggled back a bit, despite wanting to warm up.

"She's small for a goblin, even a goblin girl," the colorful man said grimly, "Probably a kid that got lost. There'll be trouble when the rest of her clan comes looking."

"They won't come for me," the gobliness said. Her interjection caused all three humans to swivel their heads and look directly at her in surprise. "And I'm not a child. I'm sixteen years of age. I'm a woman." Her voice carried the tone of a death sentence with its final declaration. The man in multicolored trousers was first to break the silence that followed.

"I see," he said, "well you'll have to forgive our ignorance. It's not often that a goblin sneaks up in the night without murder or theft being their intent, miss...?"

"Sheela," she said, "My name is Sheela."

"What's your clan?" he said heavily. She cringed.

"...Saltypinch," Sheela said, pulling the shawl tighter. Just saying the name made her want to curl up and hide.

"Ah, we'll be fine then," the man said, his voice becoming more relaxed, "They don't pose much of a danger outside of business deals, which also explains why you speak our language if I had to guess. My name is Gerhard, and this is Lebar and Nora." He gestured to the large man that had grabbed her and the woman that had covered her respectively.

"Now, why were you creeping up on us in the dead of night?" he said. Sheela's only response was to gaze into the fire. Gerhard nodded back up the road. "If I'm not much mistaken, the Saltypinch mines are only a few miles back that way. We could take you there tomorrow if you like."

"No!" Sheela said, snapping out of her daze, "No...there's nothing left. It all burned. It's all probably still burning." Gerhard licked his lips slowly and took a deep breath.

"So, not much to go back to, then," he said, opening a small metal case and withdrawing a hand-rolled cigarette. He leaned toward the fire, causing the gobliness to wince, and took a drag to light it. "Should we expect more of your people to come along?" The glowing tip of the tobacco lit the man's face menacingly as he leaned back, just outside of the circle of light. Tension crept into the faces of Lebar and Nora, and the air seemed to cool despite the warm light crackling between them all.

"I don't think so," Sheela said, deciding that truth would be the best choice, even if it was only partial truth, "I don't know if anyone else got out."

"Well then, we should be in the clear," Gerhard said, coming forward again, his face returning to friendly neutrality. The other two humans began breathing again. "Is there anywhere else we can take you? We're headed to Mirfield, as I'm sure you heard, so anywhere in that direction would be fine."

The goblin woman chewed her lip uncomfortably before responding.

"I've never left the mines before," she said, "Would Mirfield be a good place to go?"

"As good as any other," the man in colorful trousers said.

III

Days passed as the gypsy caravan ambled slowly toward its destination. Nora altered some clothes for Sheela and gave her a place to sleep. Though the gobliness was glad for the charity, the dresses felt limiting in ways that made her uncomfortable. She understood the need to fit into her new surroundings, though, and wore the clothing anyway. Most of her contribution to the group was helping cook and care for animals, however, and she was growing concerned that there had been no opportunities to do what she had actually been trained for.

Each day brought new lessons about life in the world above ground, as well as new questions about her life below. Things were so different that as much of her time was spent observing as was working, and almost all of her time working was spent in Nora's wagon.

"I appreciate the fetching and carrying," Nora said, cooking a stew for the evening meal, "but I promise we'll find something better for you eventually."

"Mm," Sheela said absentmindedly as she scrubbed inexpertly at a pile of dishes. That anyone could do this sort of work all the time amazed her.

"I mean, if you're sixteen, you'd think you would have been trained in something," said the gypsy woman.

"You'd think," said the gobliness, now actively holding back information. She did not relish the idea of sharing too much, since she was still feeling out cultural differences. However, when Nora put down her ladle and turned a stern expression on her, the small green woman sighed, knowing she could no longer escape the question.

"I was supposed to be the new shac ghuukhaar," Sheela said. It was the first time she had used her native tongue since her escape. She transitioned between the two languages smoothly. "The best translation I can give you is 'clan mother'."

"So, some kind of priestess?" Nora said, suspiciously raising an eyebrow.

"That would be a polite way of putting it," Sheela said, "It's the woman in the clan that trains other women to be 'ready' for their future husbands." She was unsure of how the other races handled intimate relations, but had made several assumptions based on how she had seen them act. The fact that all of the women she had encountered in the caravan were always clothed suggested, in her mind, that it was something they were ashamed of.

Nora looked the gobliness up and down critically, and Sheela fidgeted under the gaze. Having lived most of her life naked, being looked at was not by itself embarrassing, but the judgement she always perceived in Nora's eyes was becoming uncomfortable. She always felt as if the woman was studying her.

'A fair cop,' Sheela thought, tilting her head forward and looking at the floor with slight embarrassment, 'I'm always watching what they're doing, so of course they're watching me.' She tried to hide behind her bangs, as if it would allow her to escape the offense she was sure she had committed.

"So, more like a temple prostitute than a priestess," Nora finally said matter-of-factly. Sheela breathed a sigh of relief and nodded, but took note of the curt edge to the other woman's voice. "I take it you're considered attractive for a goblin, then?" It was an honest question, but still quite offensive.

"Of course I am!" Sheela said, stamping her foot and jutting out her lower jaw, "I might be short, even for a goblin, but I've got perfect hips and huge tits!" Looking up at the human woman, a bit of reality suddenly struck her. Though she was well-endowed for a goblin, she was actually rather average in a direct comparison to any of the larger races, despite the difference in body scale making her seem more impressive at first glance. Much of the wind drained from her sails.

"B-besides," she said, trying to recover, "I'm really flexible, I can dance well, and I had special training for...I can even do a little magic." She bit her lip again.

"Okay, okay," Nora said, smiling and holding her hands up in a disarming manner, "I didn't mean anything by it, I just don't know what goblins think looks good, okay?" She returned to stirring the pot of stew.

"Magic, though," she said, letting loose a sly, sideways look back toward the little lady, "Are we talking about levitation, hypnosis, fire? Stuff like that?"

"Not..." Sheela said, thinking back to the burning swamp, fear in her heart, "No, I'm still...learning stuff like that. I was mostly trained to do...sex stuff." Exactly as the gobliness expected, the nearby gypsy's disposition changed suddenly. She was surprised, however, that the woman was amused instead of getting angry.

"Really?!" she said, laughing boisterously, "That's really something that exists? You have got to be joking."

"No, I'm really not," Sheela said, unsure of whether she should be offended or just relieved at that point. She played nervously with the linen of the skirt Nora had given her, now even more uncomfortable and confused by the idea of clothing. The conversation had veered far from the path she expected it to take. She decided that the direct course would be best, and set aside her own questions to continue explaining.

"Women aren't expected to do much where I come from, except be mothers and please their husbands, so all of us get at least a little bit of training in it so we can heighten the experience. And, since I was supposed to be the one to train everyone else once the old matron passed on, I got to learn more than the others." She looked furtively at the floor of the cart, at a total loss for what to say next.

"Well, I don't normally go in for that sort of 'thing'. I love dance, even teach it to the others here, but that's about as racy as things should get in my opinion. But I suppose it wouldn't be right to judge how your people do things..." Nora said contemplatively, "In any case, that's in the past now. You're with us now, so we can teach you a better way. So, are you going to finish that scrubbing or what?"

The gobliness' stood still, blinking repeatedly for a moment, trying to process what had just happened. She had not expected Nora's easy acceptance of her past, but what truly caught her off guard was the fact that the woman was willing to teach her a 'better' way. After a particularly large bump in the road nearly knocked her over, though, the little lady returned to working, still deep in thought.

'What does she mean by 'not going in for that sort of thing'? Do these people not have sex? Is it a shameful thing for them? I mean, the clan reacted badly to my exploits, but that was because I decided to...'

Sheela's thought petered out as her recent memories of the result of that issue resurfaced. She threw herself into her chores to push the terrible images away.

'She's right,' the little lady thought, 'I can do whatever I want now. I can be better, whatever that means. Figuring out how things work here is more important than dwelling on the past.'

Toil filled the rest of Sheela's day. She helped out wherever she could, using each opportunity to try out new things, but did not find anything that she particularly liked. After the caravan stopped for the night, however, the people in the traveling group of entertainers came out to have a good time with one another, and she instantly felt more at home. From what the gobliness could gather, they would be passing through a small town the following day, before continuing on to Mirfield. Because the first place was so small and rural, everyone would be expected to be on good behavior while in town so as not to draw suspicion from the residents, and a party naturally ensued in order to help everyone get any misbehavior out of the way ahead of time.

Over the course of the evening, she witnessed a great many things she did not understand. Fights broke out, but then the people made up without killing each other. People danced, then ate, then danced some more, but there seemed to be no meaning to the ritual. The music was almost all merry, unlike the droning rhythms of drum and gong Sheela had heard in the past, and the bard freely belted out endless jigs using accordion and voice without any obvious reason for doing so. The gobliness was also surprised to find out that 'he' was a 'she.' Bellows forgave her fellow little lady for the mistake, as Sheela had never met a dwarf before.

"Common mistake," she said, continuing to play as they talked, "The beard throws non-dwarfs off, though I do try to keep it nicer than my brethren to help people on. Of course, you're going to get a lot of questions, too. Most goblins people see above ground are all tooth and nail, not buxom young gals!"

"Oh, I can be toothy if I want," Sheela said, finally starting to recover some of her confidence. She pulled back her lips, and gnashed her teeth in a mock threat. This caused Bellows to laugh heartily.

"I can see that," the bard said, "Make sure not to tear anything off if you get to having a little fun, yeah?" She winked knowingly.

"I hadn't ever thought of that," Sheela said, poking the fine points of her teeth with her tongue curiously.

"A girl your age and already on the road, though," the bard said, "you must have a trail of men clamoring for your hand in the places you've passed through, eh?"

Though the dwarf's expression clearly read as drunk, Sheela got the feeling that she would have been just as forward if sober. The gobliness thought back on some of the conquests she had made over the last few years. Though they had ultimately soured her people's opinion of her once she was found out, she had, in fact, amassed a great many suitors as a result.

"Yeah," she said, reminiscing about the fun she had had performing the act more than the people it had been done with, "Yeah, in a way, I guess I did." Sheela wondered when she would be able to use her skills again.

She bade Bellows farewell and continued meandering about the camp, observing the people she had begun to travel with. A large group near the dancers seemed entirely dedicated to be to drinking and flirting, though they never got anywhere with the second act, adding one more confusing item to the gobliness' list of strange behaviors.

Another, smaller group sat around a man and woman, who were performing some sort of ritual. As the man dealt out cards, the audience members leaned forward to get a better look at the small table between the pair. Reading the cards' faces, he made several declarations about the woman's future, causing the woman to gasp and go running toward what Sheela presumed was her wagon. Loud yelling from inside, followed by a man's pleading voice elicited laughter from the gathered crowd. Sheela made a note to ask about this form of magic later, as there was too much going on around the man for her to ask him at the moment.

At the edge of the camp, she heard familiar voices. Gerhard, Lebar, and Nora once more sat talking around a fire, this time joined by a lithe elf clad in fitted clothing. His blonde hair shone in the light of their small fire. The group did not appear to notice Sheela's approach.

. "So do we know where it's being kept?" the elf said, reclining against a log, spreading out like a cat.

"Well, this town isn't big enough to have a bank," Gerhard said, consulting a palm-sized leather book, "so likely the town hall. Maybe the mayor's home if he's particularly paranoid."

"A town hall would be easy," Lebar said, his chin in his hand as he thought, "but a mayor's house? Wouldn't it be guarded, even at night?"

"I doubt it," Gerhard said, shaking his head, "At least not competently."

"Well, you have options to get in, either way," Nora said.

"Looking to steal something?" Sheela said. The group turned to face her in one horrified motion. Though they had been watching along the road for safety, she realized too late that they had not been expecting to be approached from their own camp, and that she had likely broken some unspoken rule. There was a moment of tension as they exchanged looks before Gerhard filled the silence.

"'Steal' is a bit strong of a word," he said, carefully rationalizing, "We...didn't get paid much when we came through here last, so we figured we might even out the balance books in a way."

"Oh, okay," Sheela said. Taking what you wanted or needed was a time honored tradition among goblins, so the situation made complete sense to the diminutive woman. "I'll let you get back to planning, then." She turned to walk back towards the crowded center of the camp.

"Hold on, you might be helpful." Gerhard said, putting a little too much emphasis on the last word, "You ever had to 'distract' a guard, Sheela?"

"Had to? No," the gobliness said as she came back around and joined the small group around their fire, "But I have 'distracted' a few guards before." She gambled on her understanding of the caravan leader's leading question by hiking up her bosom suggestively. This evoked an incredulous look from Nora and one of curiosity from the elf, who suddenly became much more interested in the conversation.

"Well," Gerhard said, wheels turning behind his eyes as he made an addition to his plans, "I'm sure that worked quite well among your own kind, but I'm not sure-" His doubtful bait worked, and the glare from the little woman clipped his sentence short.

"Now, now," the elf said, trying to disarm the situation, " Believe it or not, not everyone thinks my kind are beautiful, and we all know what usually happens when people find out

Lebar is a half-giant." The enormous man shifted uncomfortably from side to side, his face clearly growing red with embarrassment, even in the light of the fire.

"Do we really need her to do something like that?" Nora said, "You know how I feel about using those methods."

"Nora, need I remind you that when we met, you-" Gerhard said, but found himself cut off by a woman's look for the second time in the conversation.

"Well, she can dance with the others," Nora said firmly, "I think she'll be a natural entertainer in any case, and we shouldn't push her to toward that sort of thing."

A few seconds of silence followed. The caravan leader and the gypsy woman seemed to be having a silent conversation with their eyes, but Sheela lacked any sort of context to understand the meaning. However, something had clearly happened between the two in the past, and she could not help but wonder what it might have been.

"Sheela, this is Fenian," Gerhard said, accepting that he had been overruled, and gesturing to the blonde elf, "He's one of our acrobats, but he's also good at getting into places people tend to keep locked."

"You can call me Fen," Fenian said, "I'm sure it will be enjoyable to work with you." He waggled his eyebrows a little.

'Finally, someone who's straightforward about things,' Sheela thought.

"So what is it we're taking, then?" she said, and sat down to continue the discussion long into the night.

IV

The morning was still fresh as the caravan approached its target. Away from the road, fields of grain spread over the rolling hills, interspersed with herds of animals, and Sheela watched with fascination as beasts and people worked their own form of agricultural magic. The mushroom gardens and pig styes of her life below ground were nothing compared to the majesty of wheat waving in the summer breeze, or the sight of horses frolicking in their enclosures.

Taking a deep breath, she appreciated the bounty that the world had to offer. Though she knew she would never be able to return home, the world was too breathtaking to worry about it. Even if she found herself in a place where she was not welcome, there would be more places to go, more lands to explore, and that thought made her heart flutter with excitement.

A small collection of buildings appeared among the smattering of farms that dotted the nearby countryside, forming the unnamed town's market and civic center. The caravan skirted the edge of the area, careful not to intrude when it settled down.

"Why not just drive into the square?" Sheela said to Gerhard as he walked around, checking on each wagon.

"We probably have more people in our caravan than they do living here most of the time," he said, "If we just waltzed in, it might seem like an invasion to these people, so we just do the polite thing and hold back a bit."

As performers opened their wagons up, they began rehearsing various acts for the evening. While she helped around the camp, Sheela occasionally saw eyes peeking in their direction from the windows of various buildings on the outskirts of the town, and even one person running towards the outlying plantations that she knew had to be a messenger, yet there seemed to be curiously little foot traffic near them.

"They're still trying to decide if we're welcome or not," Nora said as she gave up helping Gerhard roll a smaller cart out of his wagon. It had become jammed somehow, causing the man to swear up a storm in frustration as he struggled with it pointlessly.

"Ah," Sheela said, then took a stab in the dark, "Did they not like the show last time?"

"Considering how low our take was, I guess not," the gypsy woman said, wiping her brow and turning to the little lady with a roguish smile, "which is why we have that plan to earn a little extra this time."

As the sun rose higher in the sky, a few people went into the town to purchase supplies and gather information. Nora was leading the dancers through their basic routine, doing her best to get the inexperienced women to follow the beat and work together. Though Sheela had been instructed to learn it, she snuck off at her first opportunity, eager to explore.

'I'm not performing tonight, anyway,' she thought, assuming that the easy moves they were working on were being done for her sake, 'they'll get to rehearse a better act if I'm not around. Besides, if push comes to shove, I'll just stick to the back and keep out of sight.'

Once out of the camp and in the town, the gobliness meandered about aimlessly. By that time, she had become aware that Gerhard's group had not attacked her because she did not appear to be a threat, so she did her best to look innocent for the townspeople as well, unaware that this would have the exact opposite effect. A goblin with bright red hair wandering around the market square on the day a gypsy caravan arrived inevitably drew the attention of everyone she passed.

The First Night

Sheela kneaded absentmindedly at her skirt as she looked around. With no money, she had no way of buying anything, and so deliberately kept her hands to herself as she passed stalls of fresh food, tools, woodwork, and other products. Worst of all was the display of fabrics she came upon. The gobliness' sense of touch was extremely sensitive, and she yearned to experience every piece of material's unique feel, but knew it would cause trouble. When she saw the high price on what she considered to be a low quality gauze, she thought back to the thin scarlet silk she had tucked into a corner of Nora's wagon.

'If this passes for expensive here, then how much is my fabric worth?' she thought, and decided she would have to hide it when she had the chance. Looking up, she noticed the intense nonchalance with which the booth's owner was watching her, and moved on.

'I didn't even touch anything,' Sheela thought, 'what's her problem?'

As the gobliness neared the town hall, she slipped into the first real crowd she had seen that day. Their attention was firmly upon someone speaking in front of the rustic official building, allowing her to go largely unnoticed. The man was holding an old, but expensive-looking sword aloft.

'And there's our prize,' Sheela thought, thinking back to the previous night's discussion, and listening to the man's speech.

"...whereupon the last orc fell. He sheathed this very blade, saying 'When you are once again in danger, draw this forth, and you shall be saved.' Malik of Many Swords left us this gift, and, taking only what few supplies we could spare, set off once more into the world. Now…"

"Enjoying your rehearsals?" said a voice quietly above Sheela as the official speaker continued. She turned to see the multi-colored trousers of Gerhard, and looked up, expecting him to be angry. Instead, he wore a wry smile.

"I wanted to come see what a human town had to offer," she said, not even bothering to lie, "It's quite different. There's no fighting, and it feels bigger, even if that's only because there's sky above instead of a tunnel ceiling."

"I'm sure you could still find a fight if you wanted to, and if you think this is big, even Mirfield will give you a real shock. In any case, we should head back to the camp," the caravan leader said, inclining his head toward the speaker with the sword, "We've seen what we needed to." He started to walk away, moving with a purpose. Sheela struggled to keep up, and ultimately resorted to lifting her skirts slightly so she could run. As she bounced along the cobbles, even the moderate cut of her dress could not completely hide the moving shapes beneath her bodice and petticoat. A whistle and catcall were directed at her from somewhere along the lane.

"Alright, I was wrong," Gerard said without looking at her as they continued to move, an amused tone in his voice, "I'm still not ready to send you out on your own, but if you can get that kind of attention wearing such drab clothing, maybe I will let you dance with our ladies tonight."

Sheela smiled, and her run became even more energetic as she raced to get back to the camp.

"I'd better find something to wear, then!" she called out as she headed for Nora's wagon with all haste.

V

Over the following hours, Sheela met more of the other women in the caravan for the first time while she and her benefactor asked around for dance garments. Most of them viewed her as a curiosity, though a few of them clearly did not like the shapely little lady. Her bust and hip measurements were close enough to those of a small human woman that most of what they found could be adjusted to fit well enough with a little hemming. As a result of her upbringing, she was more than comfortable showing off her skin, and picked out the most risque outfits Nora would let her get away with. However, she refused to take anything with bells or coins used as decoration.

"That would too similar to a...ceremonial piece of clothing from back home," Sheela told Nora, a hint of embarrassment in her voice, "If I wear something like that, I have to have made it myself."

"The clothing or the coins?" the human woman said, causing Sheela to consider it for the first time.

"Both, I think," she said, after a moment of thought.

Her benefactor shrugged and seemed to accept the explanation at face value. After Nora politely eliminated a few outfits that she deemed would show too much of the gobliness' bust, they eventually decided on a pairing made of a deep purple taffeta that matched the color of Sheela's eyes near perfectly, and featured a bit of lace with topstitching in shiny thread for decoration instead of the verboten coinage common to the style.

After the little lady changed into her new performance clothes, she and Nora went to meet their co-conspirators in Gerhard's wagon. The caravan leader was the only one there when they arrived, so the gobliness began to poke around. The space was filled with a number of magical implements that she had seen before when people rehearsed their acts at night. When she began to handle them, she was quite surprised to find out that they were all cunning tricks.

"Most people can't perform real magic," Gerhard said, amused by her amazement, "so stuff like this allows us to astound crowds, even if it's just a ruse."

"Don't people get mad when they find out?" Sheela said.

"No, it's mostly understood that what happens in a show is fake," Nora said, "Everyone just sort of goes along with it because it's exciting to pretend it's real."

Sheela nodded, still playing with a set of rings that could supposedly come apart without force. She did not really understand the concept, but was willing to accept it as truth for the time being.

"Welcome, gents," Gerhard said as the door at the rear of the wagon swung open. Fenian and Lebar stepped inside as he continued to speak, "Got what you'll be needing?" Both of the men nodded.

While Fenian was still dressed quite sleekly, he patted a bulging leather pouch on a slung belt he had added to his ensemble. Metal objects clinked softly within, doubtlessly the tools he would need to retrieve the sword. Lebar, hunched over due to his great stature and the wagon's relatively low ceiling, had donned more feral looking clothes that played up the stereotypes of his giant heritage. His well-oiled muscles gleamed in the lantern light, though the intelligence in his eyes belied the costume's false nature.

"Good," Gerhard said, then looked directly at the elf with a smirk, "Fen, I'm so sad to hear that you have other business in town that will prevent you from performing with us this evening."

"I'm sure you'll make due without me," he said, going along with the joke, "Besides, I wouldn't want to steal the limelight from our newest performer." The elf winked at Sheela.

The First Night

"Well thank you for the opportunity," Sheela said, a smug look on her face. Despite Nora's earlier warnings, she had shifted the mulberry purple brassiere and skirt to expose enough of her yellow-green skin that she was pushing firmly against the boundaries of what would be acceptable in what the sandy-haired gypsy had described as a 'family friendly' performance. It was clear that the gobliness' freckles graced far more than her cheeks and shoulders, and interesting lines drawn on her skin showed just over the top of her skirt. She shook her hips in the elfen man's direction and returned his wink.

"Pretty standard show structure, otherwise," Gerhard said, ignoring the interaction, " The goal is to make this a big show to allow Fenian to deal with his business with as few interruptions as possible. Lebar will open with the other strongmen and acrobats to grab everyone's attention. The dancers will take over from there, further tantalizing the crowd."

"I know you ducked out of rehearsal early, but I think you'll do fine," Nora said to Sheela in a friendly, yet covert manner.

"Capping off the evening, Nora and I will do our 'magic' act. Any questions?" Gerhard said. The group shook their heads. "Then let's have a good show."

VI

The group, minus Fenian, joined up with the rest of the caravan's performers, who had already congregated in the middle of the camp. They all formed a line behind Bellows, who played a jovial march, and headed toward the center of town. The dancers danced and the strongmen flexed as they moved to the beat. The parade soon had a wake of residents, curious to see what the outsiders were up to, and more people were joining by the moment.

Almost all who gathered had an unintelligent look about themselves. From the state of their fields, they were clearly quite good at farming, but Sheela wondered if there was anything more to their lives. Some of the people in the crowd eyed the mixed group with suspicion, particularly the few full-breed orcs who work alongside Lebar. The gobliness thought back to the bit of story she had heard earlier in the town square, and wondered if it would have been safer for them to sit the performance out.

She also noticed that, for some reason, everyone seemed to be trying to avoid looking at her. Armed with the assumption that she just was not trying hard enough, Sheela began to move with more overt flamboyance, which only resulted in people trying more intensely to find somewhere else to look. She wanted to ask Nora what she was doing wrong, but the human woman was at the back of the train with Gerhard, pushing the colorful hand-cart filled with tricks that would be necessary for the show's final act.

As they entered the square, Bellows' changed songs, and the festive tones of her accordion filled the air with the show's overture. The acrobats fanned out, jumping, rolling, and tumbling about. They created a living barrier between the growing audience and the fountain, offering a distraction which allowed the other performers to prepare their acts with less attention on what they were doing.

Sheela fell in with the dancers, who were stretching in preparation. Though she slightly regretted ducking out of rehearsal earlier in the day, she was sure she would be able to follow along well enough not to embarrass anyone. The gobliness happily began to limber up, unaware of the dirty looks she was getting from the others as she easily bent double and touched her toes, then dropped into a split to continue loosening her muscles.

"Good evening, good evening, good evening, ladies and gentlemen," Gerhard said, his voice carrying across the open area. Bellows reduced her volume and nodded to a few other musicians, who began to pick up her tune on various wind instruments. The jugglers took the cue as well, and rubber balls formed several energetic arcs behind the man as he continued to speak.

"We humble tumblers and passionate performers are glad to display our gifts to you on this late summer evening," he said, spreading his arms wide. "Our first act tonight will be a demonstration of strength, starring the wild men of the western mountains!"

Drums began, and rose in volume, their beat becoming more intense as the rugged men stepped forward. Made up of a mixture of humans and orcs, the group all wore exaggerated grimaces and warpaint that would be utterly useless in battle, but made for good showmanship. Their appearance made some audience members visibly uncomfortable.

'Those townspeople have probably seen a raid or two,' Sheela thought, always observing, even mid-stretch.

The strongmen began to ferry objects forth, tossing heavy-looking hay bales and barrels as if they were nothing, and stacking them precisely into interesting and difficult-to-balance shapes. When one flew off course, it caught an acrobat in the back, knocking the man over.

'Well, he's out of the show,' the gobliness thought, continuing her internal commentary.

To her surprise, one of the strongmen nonchalantly retrieved the bale, and tossed it back to his compatriots, who were creating a perfectly even vertical tower. Two other tumblers lifted their fallen brother, set the man on his feet, and dusted him off. He waved to the audience to show that he was alright, then keeled over in a dramatic fashion. The earlier unrest gave way to a ripple of laughter that spread slowly as people gave in to the show, and suspended their disbelief. It dawned on Sheela that it was the first real trick of the evening, and that this was what Gerhard and Nora had been trying to explain.

'The audience doesn't want reality,' she thought, 'they've got plenty of that. They're looking for a fantasy.'

Lebar stepped forward, and the townspeople inched back. Even though they had been primed for the moment by the smaller muscle-bound men, the half-giant's stature was enough to trigger a deep-seated instinct in most people. The massive man raised his arms and roared, causing the acrobats to scatter. He grabbed one of the smaller men as he ran past, and held the clown aloft.

After the jugglers made several comedic attempts to down Lenart with their rubber balls, two of the other musclemen grabbed his arms, but he dug his heels in and lifted them with ease. Another two joined them, but again he continued to strike his threatening pose. By the third time, realization washed over the crowd, and they began to clap as more heavy men were held aloft by the half-giant.

"Lebar, man of the mountains, everyone!" Bernard said, flourishing a hand to the towering performer, who bowed his head slightly to accept his applause, then walked off, still carrying the seven other men. The music seamlessly shifted to a more sultry tune. "Next up, the dancers of the desert will beguile us with their captivating choreography."

Sheela kept to the back while they moved forward. Though she knew this would make her harder to see, the gobliness wanted to ensure that she would be able to follow along without making everyone else look bad. In a way, this was impossible.

'They're still acting all stiff,' she thought as the dance began, and tried to project her thoughts at her fellow performers, 'This is a real show, do your best!'

The group went through an easy beginning number, using the light and loose designs of their skirts to enhance the limited hip movements they were producing. From the audience's perspective, it looked impressive enough, but from a trained person's point of view, they were barely moving.

'Maybe it's another performance trick,' Sheela thought, as individuals began to step forward and perform solo, 'We do the easy stuff together, and show off our real skills on our own?'

The group moved back a little, forming a line and starting a two-step to keep moving as each person stepped forward to dance solo. Sheela kept her attention forward to the audience, but could hear the jangle of finger cymbals and coin belts moving slowly down the line as each person did their piece. Occasional hoots and catcalls from the audience seemed to support her hypothesis; this was when everyone was really giving it their all.

The little lady moved forward as the woman to her right stepped back. Swaying side to side, her body seemed to slither from head to toe. Her hair flowed out behind her, half a beat behind, and provided a mesmerizing red contrast to the green of her skin and purple of her garments. She allowed her fluid movements to extend to her arms, each one becoming a snake in its own right. They danced, intertwining and gliding around one another, parting every once in awhile to provide glimpses at her body behind.

The audience grew silent, and Sheela took this to mean that she was disappointing them. Redoubling her efforts, she rocked her hips as she began a round of quarter-turns. All of her training in dance had been aimed at showing off her form, and whereas most cultures make their dances subtly sexual, goblins made things almost entirely blatant. Each time she extended a leg, it went straight through a slit in her skirt, revealing skin all the way up to her hip. Enough of her bust and bottom were shown that there was no room to doubt that the gobliness' exaggerated features were real, and not padding.

Every time a movement popped, ephemeral bells seemed to tinkle softly in the air. Finishing her turn, Sheela spotted a man who had scowled at her mere presence earlier that day in the market, now giving her a hungry look from within the crowd.

'Ah,' the little lady thought, 'so I am doing well.'

Knowing that she had the audience's full attention made her want to continue, but Sheela could feel the eyes of the next woman in line boring into the back of her head. As she moved back, she noticed another impressed-looking face in the crowd. Fenian had appeared near the edge of the audience, a large package wrapped in cloth slung across his back. Making eye contact, he tipped his head to her, then moved away into the night.

"Give it up for our divine dancers!" Gerhard said a few solo performances later. The audience finally broke the silence Sheela's movements had cast upon them, and began to cheer and applaud.

The dancers stepped forward as one, back to moving in sync and forming a wall of attention-grabbing flesh that drew everyone's mind away from the next act setting up. Sheela kept up easily, careful not to stick out too much, lest she draw more ire from the rest of the group. When the sounds of movement ceased behind them, Bellows led a final shift of compositions, and the dancers cleared the stage.

"Our final act tonight will feature feats of magic unheard of..." Gerhard said, beginning his own act with Nora. The caravan leader's voice faded as Sheela snuck away. Just under a meter tall, it was easy for her to disappear in a crowd, even if there were eyes still on her. She did her best to follow the narrow road back to the caravan camp. Though the darkness should have scared her, a mostly safe childhood spent underground gave the gobliness an unearned sense of comfort in the poorly lit alley. Without the bright light of the sun or strong torches, the soft golden glow produced by the lines on her hips became more apparent, even showing through the fabric of her skirt slightly where it covered the marks.

"Hold it right there," an angry voice said. It contained the gravel of someone who smoked and yelled too much. Sheela was unsurprised to see that it belonged to the leering man from the crowd.

"Orcs coming into town are bad enough," he said, "but at least they're too stupid to get up to no good if they have a good master. Goblins is cunning little things, though. I don't know what kind of magic you worked on me an' me mates, but what we felt ain't natural, and I'm gonna' teach ya' not to do it again." The man cracked his knuckles in what was meant to be a menacing way.

"Oh, I haven't actually used any magic yet," Sheela said, choosing not to take the hint and raising her hands, palms up. Her expression was one of bored determination. Though the gobliness was unsure if the man were simply drunk or really was that full of hate, she was prepared to use up some more of her power to take care of the problem if she had to. As the light around her began to glow just a fraction brighter, a disarming voice rang against the cobblestones.

"That was a wonderful performance, Sheela," Fenian said, ignoring the angry man completely for the moment, "I'm glad I took the evening off to see it! Of course, I'm sure it was just as lovely from behind, where the other acrobats were."

"Thank you, Fen," she said, holding her stance, lest the angry man try anything.

"What did you think of the performance?" Fenian said, as he finally turned to the villager. His grin fought against the man's scowl until the human submitted and returned to a neutral position, though the ghost of a grimace remained.

"It was unlike anything we've ever seen 'round here," the angry man said, his tone poorly masking his ill intent, "I'm sure that sort of thing strikes some people's fancies, but we don't appreciate it 'ere." He spat on the road, and walked away. Both Fenian and Sheela watched him, unmoving, until he was out of sight.

"You really ought not to travel alone in towns," Fenian said, his eyes still fixed on where the man had gone, "Not safe, really."

"I could have taken care of him," Sheela said, lowering her hands onto her hips, the glow returning to its normal background level.

"I thought most of your magic was for pleasure," he said, his sentence lilting into an unasked question at the end.

"Most of it is," she said coyly, a smirk spreading on her lips, "Maybe that's how I was going to take care of him. Besides, why trouble yourself over me?" Though she had not actually winked, it was so heavily implied that she may as well have.

"You pique people's curiosity," he said, shrugging as if unconcerned, "and you're clearly a good distraction."

"Is that because I'm attractive?" she said, leaning forward slightly. Though her top was already cut low, the action served to create a little more cleavage. She knew how to use her weapons well.

"Yes, it's because you're attractive," Fenian said, finally joining in on the smirk.

"Then shall we adjourn to the camp to discuss things further?" the gobliness said, "Maybe share a few 'fighting' techniques?"

"Better be quick," the blond elf said, "the show will be ending soon, and then we'll have to leave town."

"Oh, don't worry," Sheela said, her expression becoming a shark-toothed, predatory grin, "I'll make it quick."

The rest of the walk back was uneventful aside from a little more flirtation. When they arrived, the two found that the caravan camp was quiet, but not unoccupied. A few people sat tending fires on guard duty, while a small group of children played off to one side. Since all of the performers were still at the show, however, the atmosphere was largely undisturbed.

"Shall we head to my wagon," Fenian said, "since you don't have your own?"

"Lead the way," Sheela said with an open-palmed gesture. She danced excitedly in the elf's wake.

'Finally,' she thought, 'a chance to recharge a little.'

Fenian's home was little more than a cart. Whereas Nora's wagon seemed designed to have lines of people move through for food, and Gerhard's was an overflowing storage for props and costumes for the whole caravan, the elfen acrobat's transport seemed to only have enough space for one person to sleep in. Perhaps two if they were very friendly.

'It'll be a tight fit,' Sheela thought, 'but that's part of the fun, I suppose.' She had a hungry look about her.

"Go ahead and have a sit," Fenian said, dropping his package and belt of tools just inside the wagon door and indicating the set of steps protruding just beneath the same, "I'm going to get a fire going."

"Okay," she said cheerily.

'Damn,' she thought, 'Won't get invited inside, then.'

Even getting up onto the stairs was a chore for the gobliness; the first step nearly came up to her waist, so she had to lift herself up onto it. She was slowly beginning to realize that the world was built in the wrong scale for people like her. After a bit of struggling, however, the little lady managed to hoist herself up in a very unladylike manner, and plopped down on the top step dejectedly.

Fenian got the fire to light after a few false starts, and Sheela did her best to hide her disappointment with being outside rather than in what would have been more personal territory. When the elf reached the wagon, however, he deftly picked the gobliness up, sat upon the narrow steps himself, and deposited her in his own lap. When she turned to look him in the face, he wore a cunning grin.

"Not enough room for both of us up here otherwise," he said.

"Oh, I see," Sheela said, Fenian's grin spreading to her face as well. She wrapped her arms around his neck, hoping to bring him a little closer, but was unable to enclose the circle due to the difference in their heights. Instead, she opted to drop her hands and place them at her sides, which put one of them close to a rather personal location on the elf. The light of the fire made it easy for the two of them to see each other, but the darkness of the night pressed in around them, and it felt as if they were all that existed in the world.

"You know, I don't think I've ever met anyone with speckled eyes before," Fenian said, never looking away from Sheela's face. One of his hands rested in the small of her back while the other lay tantalizingly on her knees.

"Aw, you noticed," Sheela said demurely, her hand moving up a bit, as if to shift to his chest. It never arrived there, instead going back down slowly, unnoticed. "Well, they're naturally the color of ripe mulberries, but they change to gold when I'm all full of magic."

"I see," he said, a sagely tone in his voice, "I take it these are connected with that as well?" The hand on her knees moved up her legs and hooked its thumb on the waistline of her skirt, pulling it away from the gobliness' body just enough to fully reveal some of the symbols embedded in her flesh. The gobliness' moved her arm enough to clear his field of view, but did not divert it from its task. The elf took a sharp breath as understanding dawned on his face.

"Did someone...carve these into you?" he said.

"Yes," she said matter-of-factly, "I did."

Each glowing symbol was made of thin lines of scar tissue. They had been cut deeply with a very sharp blade, then sewn up with great care and skill, so as to leave the very specific runic shapes necessary when they healed. Sheela smiled, proud of her work, as Fenian explored a few of them with the tips of his fingers. She concentrated on breathing evenly as her excitement grew with such a personal touch. The elf, in awe, said something in his people's lyrical language.

"I thank you for the compliment," Sheela said.

"You speak Elfen?" Fenian said, astonished.

"Yeah, Orcish too," the gobliness said, "I hung around my father's business dealings whenever I could get away with it, so I picked up a few languages after a few years."

"You are just full of surprises," the elf said, shaking his head to divert back to his original question, "but why do...this? Why not just memorize them or even have a spell book?" He looked back down at her runes, fascinated. The elfen acrobat was no longer thinking about what else was only inches further below in her skirt. He had also not noticed what she was doing, despite the growing blush on his cheeks indicating that his body was quite aware of the situation.

"They used to paint the symbols for whatever spell we were being trained in on our bodies," Sheela said, pressing his hand flat against her lower belly with her own free hand. The warmth of his palm spread through her body. "I made the argument that, since I was expected to train others, I should be allowed to make the marks more permanent, so they wouldn't rub off unexpectedly. The ruse worked for a while."

"So why did it stop...working?" Fenian said, now finding it harder to breath. Sheela's indirect suggestion seemed to work, as his hand began to move slowly back and forth along the belt of runes.

"They found the one I kept secret," she said, opening her mouth wide to reveal a symbol she had carved into the underside of her tongue. It was small, but glowed softly like the others amid the pink flesh.

"Oh?" he said, "A forbidden spell?" His pinky finger snuck a little lower as his hand continued to massage her embedded spells.

"A forbidden spell," she said, repeating his words with emphasis, "It keeps me from getting pregnant." The sentence dripped with implication.

"Ah," Fenian said as his hand ceased to move for just a split second as he processed the statement, "And why is that such a bad thing?"

"Goblin women are expected to be prolific, and the men expect to have control over when that happens," Sheela said confidently. Explaining it was empowering. "I decided that it would be my choice instead, but I like bedding people too much to give the act up, so they eventually figured out that something was going on."

"And what happened as a result?" he said. The hand on Sheela's stomach had continued to drop slowly, with only its index finger and thumb remaining on her runes. Fenian's other hand seemed torn between creeping up or down her back, instead just rubbing it absentmindedly. His face was fully flush.

"Imprisonment, trial…" she said, her eyes growing distant for a moment as she thought back to the demise of her former home, "…and now I'm here."

Raucous noises were beginning to approach the camp. Bellows' accordion was accompanied by laughter and the sounds of people discussing the performance, critiquing each other and boasting of their own deeds. Fenian sighed.

"I suppose our privacy is at an end," he said, then shuddered a little.

"For now, anyway," Sheela said sweetly, giving him a final squeeze before extracting her hand from his trousers, "I promise I'll do more for you next time." Her eyes contained more gold than before, and she licked her fingers clean. She could feel energy welling within, and reveled in the idea that he had not felt it coming.

Fenian looked down, visibly astonished that her sneak attack had been so successful, then carefully set Sheela back on the ground before hastily doing up his trousers. The gobliness adjusted her skirt to again show off just a little more of her stomach than Nora would approve of, and continued to give the elf a sly look. He was obviously flustered and on unfamiliar ground, but cleared his throat and tried admirably to regain his footing.

"Mm, indeed, we'll have to continue this discussion another time," Fenian said, still red in the cheeks when Gerhard approached them.

"Good evening, you two," the man in multicolored trousers said, amused judgement barely masked by a placid expression, "Celebrating a successful night?"

"Yes, yes," Fenian said emphatically as he retrieved the package from his cart, "my 'errand' wasn't too difficult. Sheela and I were discussing her...performance"

"And a good one it was, especially for a first timer," Gerhard said honestly, "try not to make too many enemies of the other ladies, though." He winked at her, took the cloth-covered box from Fenian, then slapped the elf on the arm with a smile.

"Now stop acting like an embarrassed child," he said, "You're older than I am, man! You can make your own choices, it's no business of mine. But wrap it up quick, we need to leave. Wouldn't want the townspeople to catch on before we have enough road between us and them." He touched the end of the long box to his head in a mock salute and headed off into the night.

Fenian had a sour look as he tossed sand at the fire, then stamped it out. Turning back to his wagon, he was greeted with Sheela, her hands on her hips and one eyebrow cocked up.

"Seriously?" she said, "Given how you acted before, I figured you would've been ready and happy for a little 'manual stimulation'."

"You just caught me off guard is all," he said, a touch of anger in his voice, "It won't happen next time." The elf's face made it clear that there was something else he was not saying.

"Oh, next time?" Sheela said, choosing to ignore the subtext of his expression, "We'll see, if that ever happens."

"Wha- but you said-" Fenian said, a shocked, pleading expression on his face.

"For now, good night," the gobliness said, a teasing cadence in her voice as she sashayed away. The ephemeral bells seemed to jingle anew as she walked.

'So this is what it's like to really be in control of my own life,' she thought, pleased with the feeling.

VII

The caravan packed up quickly and, for the first time since Sheela had joined it, traveled through the night. Though only a select few knew what had actually transpired in the town, everyone moved with haste when Gerhard told them they needed to. Horses and oxen puffed their complaints occasionally, but were urged on with either treats or lashes, depending on their disposition. Nora was driving her own beasts, not wanting to trust them to someone else under the circumstances.

Sheela spent the first part of the evening looking for places to hide her bundle of material. The sheer fabric had been cleaned since her mad dash, and it was once more a brilliant scarlet. Eventually, she realized that nowhere in the cart would remain hidden, since it was really Nora's home, not her own. The gobliness chewed her lip in contemplation, then poked her head out one of the windows at the fore of the wagon.

"Hey Nora," she said, "is there any chance you have a spare rucksack? I don't care if it's fabric or leather, I'd just like to have one."

"I don't think I do, sorry," Nora said, keeping her eyes on the cart ahead of them, "but you could buy one in Mirfield when we get there."

"I don't have any money," Sheela said, confused.

"Well, you performed, so you'll get a little pay," the human woman said.

"Oh, right," the little lady said, then changed tacks, "Then do you have any scratch paper and something to write with?"

"Yeah, should have some somewhere in the chest of drawers," Nora said.

"Thanks," Sheela said.

She pushed a stool over to the chest and climbed it to be able to see its contents instead of groping around in the drawers blindly from below. Paper was easy enough to find, though it was cheap and thin. Sheela eventually gave up on finding a proper pen, opting instead to use a charcoal stylus that had smudged up a corner of one of the drawers. Just handling it turned her fingers black.

Hopping down from her vantage point, she spread the paper on the open floor and laid down in front of it. She began to sketch out a traditional garment similar to those worn by the other dancers, but much more ornate by design. Instead of a few coins here and there, much of its surface was encrusted in them. The embroidery or lace commonly used to accent the brassiere was replaced by semi-circular gold frames that, at some point in goblin history, had been meant to give a woman's chest some support, but really just accented her assets. Other small loops represented bracelets and rings wrought from the same gold.

Almost none of this was actually clear from the crude drawing, but the sketch merely served as a way for Sheela to exercise her imagination. As her thoughts flowed randomly, she began to doodle other things; two small female figures in front of a boxy shape were her and Nora by the wagon, a dark face with glowing eyes and mouth for the Saltypinch mines, and scant random lines that might one day become new runes.

As she drew, the wagon bumped and rumbled along the road, lead and followed by more of its kind as the caravan headed toward Mirfield. Eventually, her eyelids drooped as the motion rocked her to sleep.

A restful night's sleep later, Sheela woke with a start when the wagon stopped. Her drawing stuck to her face as she sat up. Pulling it off, she was glad to see it wasn't too badly smudged, but knew she would have charcoal on her face nonetheless. She blinked a few times, stretched and yawned, then tried to get water from the barrel near the stove. Greeted by only a trickle, she used the little bit to wash her face and hand, then used the stool to once again climb to a height that would be considered normal for a taller race. Opening the top of the cask, she could see that its level had fallen just below the tap.

Looking outside once again, she did not see Nora in the seat behind the pack animals. Going to the door at the back of the wagon, Sheela found the woman bringing in wood she had gathered from the nearby forest. Nora gave her an amused look when she caught sight of the gobliness.

"Still haven't changed out of your dance clothes, eh?" she said.

"I like them," Sheela said, furrowing her brow a little, "Why would I change out of them?"

"To do some chores, maybe?" Nora said, still smiling.

"That reminds me, the water barrel is almost empty," the gobliness said.

"Then you'll really want to get changed," the gypsy woman said, "I heard a river somewhere to the North when I was in the forest. You can take a bucket and get some more."

"Alright," Sheela said, a slight sigh at the end.

"Be quick, though," Nora said, "Gerhard wants to keep going, but we had to stop for a bit to let the animals rest."

The only bucket Sheela could find was half as big as she was. Nora told her not to worry about it, so she headed out into the forest, arms wrapped around the wooden vessel, eyes and nose peeking out over its rim. Walking carefully, and tilting her head to the side occasionally so as to see the ground in front of her, the gobliness carefully searched for the river she had been told of.

Sounds of life filled the forest. Birds warned each other out of their own territory, rodents munched quietly at their breakfasts, and unknown creatures tried to be inconspicuous in the undergrowth. A rustling of leaves gave Sheela momentary pause, taking her back to that recent night in the forest. She closed her eyes and breathed slowly, calming herself, and concentrating to find the sound of running water. It babbled somewhere in the distance, the noise flowing around the trees, and coming back to her from all directions. Following where she thought it sounded loudest, she continued her trek.

Before long, she saw a few sprays of water and heard a familiar voice. Water splashed high over a large, flat stone sat in the middle of the flow. It was just high enough to poke over the surface of what was really only a stream as long as it was not flooded. Sitting on the stone, completely soaked by the random sprays was Fenian. Sheela almost snorted as she suppressed a laugh.

"Yes, ha ha, it's very funny," he said, displeased. His light hair was darkened by the water, and clumped together in strands. Meanwhile, his nice white shirt had become almost see-through and was stuck to his body.

"What are you even doing here?" she said, successfully reducing her amusement to a mere broad smile.

"Trying to be romantic," he said with a look of defeat.

As the elf was nearly knocked off the rock by a particularly large wave, Sheela could no longer contain herself; she dropped the bucket and doubled up with laughter. His look turned to a glare as she tried to regain her composure.

"Just get out of the water, you foolish acrobat," she said, taking deep breaths to calm herself, "And what is 'romantic' anyway? Please don't tell me you're trying to woo me or something." Her hands alighted on her hips, but her face was still softly amused.

"You don't know-," Fenian said as he walked through the knee-deep water to the river's edge, stopping when he remembered how restrictively she had described her culture, "Well, basically, yeah. Most of the people I've ever been with needed at least a little bit of...well, 'convincing' sounds uncouth, but you get the idea. They weren't so forward."

Sheela sighed, shook her head, and patted the dripping man on the leg.

"Well stop it," she said, "I'm not looking for anything serious, but I'll be very clear when I want something else." She squeezed his thigh for good measure.

"You are a very strange woman," he said.

"No, I just know what I want, and I'm not ashamed to ask for it," the little lady said, "Now, you should get out of those wet clothes, but I fear the caravan would leave before we got finished with the results of such an action. Would you mind helping me with the water instead, and we'll continue this jaunt another time?"

"No subtlety at all," Fenian said with an impressed look as he took the bucket and filled it from the river.

"I can be subtle if I want, I just don't play games with it," Sheela said.

'Unless it suits my needs,' she thought.

"How did you get here before me, anyway?" she said, walking ahead of the elf.

"Nora told me where you were headed after you left," he said, "and you don't exactly move quickly. Or softly, I might add."

She could feel him looking at her bottom without even checking behind herself.

"Well, I have short legs, can you really blame me for walking slower than you usually do?" Sheela said, enjoying the attention, and adding a bit more wiggle to her step for his entertainment.

"No, not at all," Fenian said, still staring, "And it's not too much trouble to take things slower sometimes."

"Oh, I have no intention of 'taking things slowly'," she said nonchalantly.

"Wha-" he said, tripping and nearly upending the bucket of water. Sheela laughed, but played nice the rest of the way back to the caravan, so as not to make anyone wait longer than necessary.

Over the rest of the trip toward Mirfield, Sheela flirted mercilessly with Fenian, but never gave him a chance to take things further. Though she yearned to do so herself, she was having too much fun with the new experience. The men in her clan had always been too aggressive, so she was used to taking care of them quickly to fulfill her own needs without incurring their wrath. Fen, on the other hand, seemed to enjoy the chase, and knowing this made it fun for Sheela as well.

VIII

The town of Mirfield could be heard soon after it was seen. Large buildings made of stone echoed the sounds of crowds in the streets, and Sheela's sharp ears could tell that all kinds of lives were being lived there. Anger, happiness, sadness, and surprise all filtered up into the air, filling the gobliness once more with the excitement of discovery as they rolled into the small city. Unlike in the unnamed farming town, the caravan fit right in among the relatively busy traffic of the crowded streets.

Sheela found herself unable to look away from the wagon's window as they slowly ambled along. On top of the stalls she had expected to see, real shops lined the path, their windows full of products from metalwork to clothing, and even one just for sweets. As they approached a particularly noisy building festooned in bright colors, the gobliness caught sight of a few scantily clad people of various races. Behind them hung posters with cheery pictures and words like "Dragon's Breath" and "New: Oorod's Ale", but she was too interested in what the group was doing to take note of the advertisements.

Men and women alike stood on the street corner, much more exposed that almost everyone else Sheela had met on the surface so far. They flirted constantly with passers-by, and occasionally one would go off with someone, often a customer coming out of the noisy building. Nora stopped reading, and joined Sheela at the window, a quizzical look on her face.

"What're you looking at?" she said, "Oh, that's a tavern. People go there to eat and drink, and some of them have rooms for rent."

"No," Sheela said, bouncing a little, "The people out front! They look like fun!" Nora's attention shifted to the group propositioning customers.

"Oh, of course that's what caught your attention," Nora said with a disappointed tone, shaking her head slightly from side to side, "They're prostitutes, Sheela. Dancing is one thing, but that's out of the question."

"But, you described me as a 'temple prostitute' when we first talked about my training," the gobliness said, tilting her head to the side in confusion, "and that didn't sound like a bad thing, so what's the difference?"

"W-well, if you served in a temple, that's by the will of a god. It's an act of worship, you see," the sandy-haired woman said, then gestured to the group they were passing, "Those people just do it for money. There's no love or devotion there."

"They get paid for sex?!" Sheela said, plastering herself against the window. She tried to take in everything she possibly could about the group before the wagon moved too far to see them. Nora sighed.

"Look, it's dangerous work and a lot of people look down on it," she said, shaking her head again, "You could get hurt if someone is too rough, or even if they just decide they don't like you. It's not safe." Her voice carried a hint of memory.

None of her warnings reached Sheela, however. The gobliness was too wrapped up in the idea that what she had spent her whole life training to do was actually a tradable skill, not just a necessity of life. Her mind whirled as she worked through everything it meant.

'I'll never have to worry about not having enough magic,' she thought, 'And I bet they never have to look very hard for a place to sleep. And the money I could make…' She blinked as another realization hit her.

"Nora, how much money is a lot of money?" the little lady said.

"What?" Nora said, taken aback by the sudden change of subject.

"I mean, I understand the idea of trade," Sheela said, "but I don't know what a good price is in your...well, I guess 'our' currency. I've never had to buy anything with it."

"You really haven't had much life experience, have you?" the gypsy said.

Sheela shook her head, then waited for an answer.

"Well, uh...I'd never pay more than five silver for a reasonable room at an inn. Maybe I'd go as high as two gold if it was a really good room..." she said, a hand on her chin as she looked into the middle distance while she thought, "Oh, you said you were going to buy a bag, right? A really nice one of those would cost you two gold, too."

"Why does a night in a really nice room cost as much as a good bag?" the gobliness said, furrowing her brow, "The bag will last a lot longer, so that doesn't make sense."

"Well, for starters, not everybody always has a place to go back to," Nora said, "and I did say a good room. Plus, someone has to take care of that room, and they need to get paid. Then there's supplies and things that need to get replaced."

"...and those need to be purchased, too. Everyone needs to make a profit," Sheela said, nodding as she caught on, "Okay, that's just how money works, though. What do I do if I think someone isn't giving me a good price? I know my father haggled with people who were buying things from the clan, but negotiations between goblins were always a little more confrontational than I'd imagine would be allowed up here."

"Well, you could do things that way, but you'll cause more trouble than it's worth. Just try to talk them down, and if you feel like they're not going to budge, just don't buy from them," the taller woman said with a shrug, "You can find almost everything in more than one place, so if you don't like it, look somewhere else."

"That sounds much easier," the gobliness said, searching the folds of her bundle of fabric for the coins she had stashed there.

"I find it difficult to believe you already understand money, but don't know how to negotiate…" Nora said.

"Oh, I'm aware of the concept, though I didn't know the word," Sheela said, "But like I said, most goblin 'negotiates' involved a lot of fighting. I just wanted to know how your people handle it." She finally extracts her pay, then tucks it into the neckline of her bodice.

"That makes sense," Nora said, picking her book back up, "And I think it should be 'negotiations' if you're going to use it like that."

"Right, of course, thank you," the gobliness said after a moment of consideration. Though she knew the basics of many languages, new words and conjugation still sometimes caught her unaware.

Below ground, her natural intelligence had given her a leg up on those around her. Above ground, in the world at large, she had come to rely on it to stay safe. After Fenian was taken by surprise that night at the fire, she asked around about how many languages people knew. The little lady was quite shocked to find out that being able to not only speak, but also read more than one was uncommon, despite the fact that everyone seemed to be in some sort of business that meant they would inevitably interact with someone who did not speak their native tongue eventually.

"At least the idiots in my clan never talked to outsiders," she said quietly to herself in the harsh goblin language, not realizing she was speaking aloud, "What's everyone else's excuse?"

"Hm?" Nora said, looking up again with a perturbed expression.

"Sorry, just thinking out loud," Sheela said, playing it off with a smile, "Do you know when we'll be stopping?"

"Should be there soon," Nora said, leaning slightly to look out one of the windows.

The caravan pulled into a large open area near the town's market. Though Sheela could see that Mirfield continued all the way around the edge of it, the space seemed big enough to accommodate an entire town in and of itself. There were no buildings or trees in the immense flat space, and nothing around it had windows facing in.

"Why in the world is there this big of an open area right in the middle of a town?" Sheela said, "Is it a religious thing?"

"That's an odd thing to say," Nora said, laughing.

"Well, the mines had this huge open cavern with a statue of Dhegaan in it that they worshipped," the gobliness said pensively, "He's the goblin deity of fire." She blinked and looked off into the distance for a split second as the irony of her old home's final fate struck her.

"That 'they' worshipped?" the gypsy said, missing the connection.

"Yeah, I never really bought into it," Sheela said, returning to the present, "His teachings said I was powerless, but I knew that wasn't true. My power was just something they didn't teach us was a power." She returns to the licentious grin she had had when she saw the prostitutes.

"Well, nobody worships here, except maybe some business people," Nora said, shrugging, "This is a Willforge landing zone. If it were here, the floating city would take up all of this open space."

"Floating...city?" the little lady said. Her eyes were wide in amazement.

"Yeah," the taller woman said, "Magic or machinery, I don't know what keeps it in the air, but it really does have amazing things. They travel the world, and even sometimes the planes, so their market has a huge variety of products, and the very best of everything. And there are people of every race that call it home, but it's also very dangerous because of the problems that causes, I hear."

"So you've never been?" Sheela said, the wheels in her brain already turning.

"No, never inside, anyway," Nora said as the wagon came to a stop, "Whenever we're near it, we send a cart or two inside to see what we can get for what we have to sell, but we've never all gone in. They keep a pretty tight border, so it would be a hassle to get everyone through. Plus, they'd either try to tax us for some of our stuff, or just take it from us."

"They sound fun," Sheela said, not fully paying attention and already heading for the door, "Well, anyway, thanks for answering my questions. Any time I should be back?"

"Just be back by sundown," Nora said, leaning back into the wagon fully and closing the window, "We should be here for a while, so don't worry about rushing. Seriously, don't cause any trouble while you're out, though!"

"I'd like to promise that," the gobliness said as she walked out with a shark-toothed grin, "but that'd be lying."

IX

As Sheela explored the city, nobody paid her any mind. At first, she was happy with this, because it felt like she was just another person for the first time in as long as she could remember. After about an hour, however, she grew increasingly aggravated with it. The little lady was used to being looked at, for better or for worse. Whether it was because of her race, her particularly small stature, or because of the rather plain dress Nora insisted she wear when not performing, the lack of attention began to feel draining on Sheela's spirit.

In this state, Mirfield's crowded streets quickly became overwhelming for the little lady. The wide variety of shops that accompanied its status as a Willforge landing place meant that every window featured items she had never seen before, from exotic weapons to animal meats with names she could not pronounce without a few attempts. It did not take long for her to find a smith who sold leather goods. The front section of the workshop had bins filled with basic products meant to accessorize any set of armor. Using a small crate as a stepladder, Sheela worked her way around the selection until she found something that was about the right size to be a ruck for someone of her stature.

"How much is this bag?" she said. The loud banging of hammer on heated metal continued to ring in her ears. It caused such pounding changes in the air pressure that each strike was almost physically painful.

"Hello?" she said, cupping her hands around her mouth in an attempt to be heard.

When she still received no response, she jumped up and down impatiently, and huffed. The hammer stopped momentarily, then continued a few more times. A rush of steam issued forth from the forge area, followed shortly by a rotund man whose moustache nearly hid his mouth entirely. His moving jaw assured the observer that it was there, somewhere beneath the facial hair, working away at something tough as he spoke.

"What can I get you?" he said. While the smith's tone was gruff, it was not totally off-putting. "Looking to buy a gift for your master, little lady?"

"No, I just wanted to know how much this bag would be," Sheela said, holding up what was meant to be a belt pouch for a large man.

"That thing won't fit on you at all," the smith said, raising an eyebrow and becoming annoyed, "There's plenty of other places that sell all kinds of frilly things, so get!" He waved a hand in her general direction and started back toward his forge. Sheela narrowed her eyes and put on a resolute expression.

"Just the same, how much is this one?" she said. Nobody had ever outdone her when it came to stubbornness, and the gobliness was determined not to let that change. The smith rubbed his neck, sighed heavily, and turned back around.

"It costs a gold," he said, "but it really won't fit you. You can't even wear a belt big enough for it to go on."

"I want to wear it on my back," Sheela said, still wearing a firm countenance.

The stout man took the bag and turned it over a few times in his hands, still chewing on his unseen mouthful as he thought.

"For an extra gold, I could see to putting some straps on it," he said, "I guess."

"Two gold is as much as a big rucksack would cost for someone your size," the gobliness said, crossing her arms over her waist, "Surely, you can do better than that."

She slowly lifted, trying a ploy that had often worked in her favor when negotiating with her clanmates. Despite her dress reducing the effect, she was able to get a little bit of heft out of her bosom. Even if her assets were average sized by human standards, the difference in scale caused by her otherwise very petite form made the act impressive. The smith's eyebrow twitched almost imperceptibly, and he chewed whatever was in his mouth a little harder.

"Alright, but I have to charge you for materials, at least," he said, "One gold and five coppers?"

"Sounds good," Sheela said, producing her shark-like smile. She paid the man, making a show of extracting the money from her bodice, and a few minutes later was handed the converted ruck.

"Thank you," she said, batting her eyes a couple of times for good measure.

"Mm," the smith said, grumbling as he walked away, "Still don't understand why a good looking girl like you'd want that, but..."

Sheela watched him go for a moment, then continued on her way, glad to know that the same tricks would work above ground as below. Though the bag had not been intended to be worn on the back, it fit her well enough, and was made of a tough leather with a solid metal clasp. As opposed to the more stylish examples she had seen in a number of shop windows, she had faith that the bag would actually last a while in a life on the road.

As she explored, the gobliness began to notice similar things to what the smith had done for her in more and more places. Not only did people seem not to have the same aversion to her as they had had in the other town, they often even tailored their services to her when she showed interest. The idea that a business could change what it offered depending on the customer intrigued the little lady, especially whenever she found a specialty shop. Still, she wondered how those survived while selling only one type of product. The most egregious of them was a thread store, its windows filled with every color of string imaginable.

"Good...afternoon," the shop owner said, glancing at a clock beside the entranceway as Sheela entered, "What can I do for you today?" The ample woman wore clothing that was a bit too small for someone of her magnitude, as well as an amount of makeup that made the little lady question whether the plump woman's face was even close to the complexion it appeared to be.

"Hi," Sheela said, surprised to be acknowledged so quickly, "I'm just looking around. I didn't expect to find a shop selling this kind of product, to be honest."

"Oh?" the woman said, "Well, there are a few of us around, though I believe my storefront is the most respectable." She had to lean forward on the countertop to continue seeing the gobliness as the little lady approached her. This resulted in the overabundant woman depositing a veritable puddle of her busty flesh upon the flat surface. She took a drag off of a long brass pipe, and the smoke that filled the air was the aromatic equivalent of a mental fog that the gobliness felt was quite familiar, but could not nail down.

"Do you do a lot of business?" Sheela said. Her suspicions were raised, but she was not entirely sure what the shop keeper's game was. The woman clearly had money, or liked it to appear that she did, but there was a bit more dust on the shelves than seemed reasonable for a profitable shop that was moving merchandise.

"Oh, yes," the woman said, "in addition to the lovely thread you see here, we offer quick clothing alteration while you wait. Our seamstresses and tailors are known to be the best in the city, and our customers always leave satisfied. Could I interest you in their services? That dress looks awfully uncomfortable."

The shopkeeper watched the gobliness closely, waiting like a cougar who had met another predator to see whether a fight would ensue or they would go their separate ways. While awaiting the outcome, she took another drag from her pipe, releasing the pungent smoke into the air once more. Sheela's memory finally kicked into gear, and images of the training room in which she had learned most of her techniques flashed through her mind. The smoke tasted like that produced by the herbs used to heighten the trainee's sense of touch. Suddenly, the nature of the shop was entirely clear.

"No, I think I'm good for now," Sheela said, more comfortable now that she knew the rules, "though I would prefer to be dressed quite...differently." Subtlety had never been her strong suit, but she knew she needed to at least try in this case.

"Oh?" the shopkeeper said, her expression unchanging, "Perhaps I can suggest somewhere to get something more fitting. What line of work are you in?"

"I suppose you could say I'm a dancer," the gobliness said, "but I'm better trained for more 'personal' services."

The shopkeeper tapped her pipe out into a stone basin and leaned forward again, giving Sheela a critical examination. Her pudgy face was still far away from the little lady, but seemed to fill the whole world. The judgement being directed at the gobliness felt similar to that Nora had expressed when they had spoken on the subject, but as if it were somehow coming from the other side of a coin. It occurred to Sheela that she had not seen another goblin over the last few weeks, so she decided it was alright to be considered an oddity worthy of examination, given the circumstances.

"Not sure I can hire on any more 'seamstresses' right now," the enormous woman said, looking directly at the little lady's chest, "but you obviously have at least a couple of 'talents', so I might see to giving you some work at some point in the future."

"Would it be stable?" Sheela said, images of the people standing on the street in front of the bar and Nora's warnings crossing her mind, "I've seen a few freelance...workers offering their services on the streets, and-"

"You would do nothing of the sort," the shopkeeper said, sitting up and scoffing, "We provide all of our workers with appropriate lodgings and materials to ensure the quality of their work. This is, of course, why we must be discerning in who we hire." She began to stuff more of the arousing herbs into her pipe.

"Oh, of course," the diminutive gobliness said, "Quality is key, otherwise you might not be the best in town anymore."

"Indeed," the woman said, nodding slowly, "I'm glad you understand. Please, stop by some other time. I'll ask around to see if there might be a space for someone with your 'abilities'."

Sheela bowed slightly, and exited the shop filled with the hopeful knowledge that there was a place for people like her in the world after all.

Outside once more, the afternoon dragged on as the gobliness continued to tour Mirfield. She meandered about, drinking in the culture of her new surroundings. Though things had been energetic in the morning, a post-noon slump seemed to have hit the whole city. People still walked about, working, shopping, and visiting friends, but the heat of the day seemed to be slowing everyone down. Sheela found herself drawn to the promise of refreshment in a building similar to the lively one she had seen as they entered the city.

The tavern was mostly lit with dim torches instead of the sunlight she had enjoyed in the other businesses she had visited, despite the presence of small windows near the top of the exterior walls. Despite this, she could tell that it was painted as colorfully inside as it was outside, even in the poor light. As opposed to the sullen warrens of the mines from which she came, the cheerful atmosphere of the building seemed to encourage happiness and jocularity in its patrons. Though tired by the day's exploration, she was uplifted by the joy in the room. The little lady ordered a drink, then quietly found a table in the corner to observe from. Around her, people talked with friends, played various games, and generally caroused.

'I can see why people come to places like this,' Sheela thought, 'So much fun to be had in one place.'

The familiar harmonics of an accordion rose just above the crowd noise, causing the gobliness' ears to perk up. She hoped to see Bellows somewhere in the crowd, but found the instrument being played by sun-tanned man in another corner of the room. Dodging randomly thrown objects seemed to be part of his act, and he usually managed to avoid any serious threats. While the gobliness laughed at his jester-like capering, a lean orc took up a seat next to her.

"Hello, little one," he said, speaking without a lisp despite his tusks, "What brings you here?" The orc sat with his back to the wall, nonchalantly keeping an eye on the rest of the crowd while also giving Sheela his attention.

"Just came into town on a caravan," she said, "You?"

"Ah, a traveler, then," he said, smoothing a stray black hair out of his face, "I wondered. Not many of our kind here. Not enough warehouse or servant jobs to go around. I'm lucky enough to have the former, and my guess for you would be that you're looking for the latter."

The man seemed much more educated and refined than the majority of the orcs Sheela had seen. However, she realized that much of her experience with them had likely been skewed by seeing them only out in the country, away from towns, or in the caravan's overly stereotypical show.

"You know, you're the second person today to assume I'm a servant," the little lady said, "Is that really the first thing people assume of goblins around here?" She took a sip of her drink in an attempt to not seem too off-putting.

"Well, servant or slave," the lean orc said, taking a drink from his own cup, "Otherwise, most of our kind stay away from towns around here. People outside of Mirfield still remember the raids that used to happen, so it's more trouble than it's worth to most."

"'Our kind'?" Sheela said, "I know goblins and orcs are supposed to be distantly related, but you make it seem like we're totally different from everyone else."

"Well, aren't we?" he said, "Our skin, our teeth, and our hair are the easy things to point out, but even our cultures are so different that some people don't trust us because of it. They don't understand how we can be proud of where we came from, even if there is some bad blood."

"I don't know what your people are like," the gobliness said, snorting and becoming indignant, "but mine expected me to become a brood sow who taught other women to be the same. I'm sure your culture is nicer, but mine can piss right off." She took in a long draught in order to prevent more anger from coming forth.

The raw emotion struck the orc without warning. He looked at her, then stared at his drink for a few moments before finally turning back to her with an apologetic expression.

"I'm sorry," he said, "Women in my tribe are traditionally warriors, same as the men, so I assumed...well, I was wrong, and I'm sorry."

"Mmhm," Sheela said.

"I'm Adelwolf," he said, "but most people call me 'Wolf'."

Sheela gave the man a sideways glance, scanning him up and down. Though she did not doubt that he came from a warrior tradition, the skinny man did not seem to fit the name he had given.

"Do people call you that," she said, a suspicious tone in her voice, "or do you want people to call you that?"

"Fair enough," Wolf said, laughing bitterly, "I like it when people call me that. Surely, having such a bad relationship with your past, you understand wanting a chance to be someone new?"

'He has a point,' Sheela thought, 'A different name would be a good way to break away from everything that's happened.' She took another long draught as she thought, finishing off her drink. It gave her enough time to come up with something.

"Then I guess you can call me 'Lilah'," she said, trying out the moniker. It fit well enough in her mouth.

"Well then, 'Lilah', let me buy you another drink," Wolf said, "I have to go to work soon, but I'd hate to leave on a bad note."

Despite what he said, the two sat and talked for a further hour. The gobliness used that time to carefully pull any information about the city out of the orc that she could, finding out more about what made the small burg tick. She found that the more drink the man had in him, the more hopeful and talkative he became.

"So is there anything else that makes Mirfield special?" Sheela said, "I mean, you've told me about how great business is here, and about some of the festivals, but I've seen more people from different races interacting than anywhere else I've been." She pointedly left out that she had only been about three places in her life.

"If you think this place is integrated, you should check out Willforge, but I'll come back to that," Wolf said, "This place actually used to be a fortress. You can still see the old wall, but now it's only really a border between older buildings and new. In the old days, it was the only place around that survived our pe- sorry, my people's roaming warbands without much of a scratch."

"Really?" the gobliness said, leaning on her hand in amusement, "I find it hard to believe you lot would be stopped by something so small as a wall."

"Well, we didn't exactly have the resources to build siege equipment," the lean orc said with a shrug, "which actually ties into what made things change. As the rest of the world moved on, developing better magic and technology, we were just kind of...left in the dust. So eventually, tribe by tribe, we starting making peace with people. Now we do a lot of manual labor jobs or bodyguarding."

"And everyone just sort of went along with this?" Sheela said, leading him on and simply letting him talk. She felt like he enjoyed that more than having the company of a female.

'More than one way to entertain, I suppose,' she thought, filing the idea away for later consideration.

"Oh, obviously not," Wolf said, ordering more drinks with a wave of his hand, "There's still a lot of racism, and it goes both ways. Plus, now there're greenskins that hate other greenskins because they 'don't uphold tradition'."

"I've heard that part before," the gobliness said with a sad laugh.

"Then you get my point," the orc said, "But, on the whole, things're better now. We have more opportunities, and I get the feeling that all of the races can gain something from working together. We've all got something to offer, you know?"

Sheela nodded in understanding. As the narrow bands of sunlight coming through the small windows above moved across the floor, however, he finally stood to leave.

"It was nice, but I really must be going," he said, teetering a little.

"Will you be okay to work?" she said. The little lady had been careful to drink slowly, not wanting to get caught drunk in an unfamiliar place. "You wouldn't want to get hurt because of something stupid."

"S'fine," Wolf said, "You have a good evening, 'Lilah'."

"You too, 'Wolf'," Sheela said, still amused by the idea of a false identity.

The orc paid both his tab and hers, then left. She followed shortly after, having grown bored with the continuous party without anyone to talk to.

X

Making her way back toward the caravan, the little lady found that the city became a different beast at night. While torches burned nearly everywhere, their light could not reach all corners of the streets and alleyways, and lurking in the shadows were the people too unwanted to come out in the glare of day. Beggars, scavengers, and other ragged looking people emerged from their various hiding places to make their meager living cleaning up the detritus of the day.

Though these people did not look at her, Sheela quickly realized it was for a totally new reason. Whereas others who had ignored her had an air of disdain about them, these people held only despair. It made the gobliness' heart ache, her mind writing stories for each one she saw as she continued to walk. Fear crept in when she realized that she was, herself, only a hair shy of their situation.

'I don't care about what Nora said,' the little lady thought as a real goal resolved in her mind, 'I have a skill, and now I know I can use it to make a living here. I won't end up like these people.'

The atmosphere of sadness seemed to scatter away from the lively gathering of wagons in the clearing, though its taint remained in Sheela's heart, even as she approached the jovial collection of people. Once more, the sound of an accordion hummed over the chatter of conversation, this time reassuringly joined by the familiar voice of the group's dwarfen bard. Sheela smiled; having another person her size around was somehow reassuring.

No rehearsing was happening that night. Even the most dedicated performers were taking the evening off to live it up on the copious supplies bought in the larger city. Unlike out in the country, where too much light at night might attract unwanted attention, the sconces of each wagon had lit torches in them, creating new alleyways and paths that seemed a natural extension of the city's own. The gobliness followed the sound of music to a place where the wagons created a loose circle surrounding a bonfire.

People sat or danced around the scene, casting long shadows in the light of the high flames. Sheela's heartbeat accelerated with reflexive fright at the sight, and she quietly skirted the edge of the ring, avoiding the celebrants along the way. Catching sight of Bellows, she made a beeline for the dwarf and practically hid amongst the pile of boxes and crates the musician was seated upon.

"What's wrong, Sheela?" Bellows said, still playing her instrument merrily, despite the face of concern she wore.

"I just got caught by surprise is all," Sheela said, "The fire just...and there were some people in town..."

"You weren't hurt, were you?" the dwarfess said.

Sheela shook her head, but her eyes still looked at something miles away.

"Okay, well, you just rest there, then. We'll talk a bit later."

The evening crawled by, and Sheela spent most of it curled up, leaning against her wooden hiding place, trying to control her breathing. She cursed herself for her weakness, but could not clear the images of destitution and destruction from her mind. As the moon rose, the fire burned lower, eventually providing only just a hair of warmth, only lighting the night when the wind fanned its dying embers. When the final audience members wandered off, Bellows put down her accordion, and turned to face the half-asleep gobliness.

"So, what's going on?" she said, undoing the braids in her beard and producing a brush from the pouch on her belt, "And take it slow."

Sheela took a deep breath and looked up at the musician. She had tears in her eyes, but the rest of her face looked angry.

"I'm scared of stupid things, and I hate it," she said, then buried her face in her knees, causing Bellows to sigh.

"You're going to have to give me more to work with than that, you know," Bellows said, her face remaining placid.

"Nora said what I'm good at isn't a good thing to be good at, but I don't want to become a beggar," Sheela said, her voice slightly muffled by her position, "And the fire just brought back so many memories…"

The dwarfess sighed once more, stopped brushing, and scooted closer to the goblin woman to rub her back.

"Well, the fire I understand, given how you came to us," she said, "but you're a really good dancer. With Nora being the one who teaches our other girls to dance, I'm quite surprised she had anything negative to say about it."

"I'm not a dancer, though," the gobliness said, sniffling slightly.

"Really? You had me fooled," Bellows said, "So, what are you, then?"

"When I told her about what I can do a few weeks ago, she said I was a 'temple prostitute'," Sheela said, finally looking up with a pout at the musician, "but then earlier today, she said being a prostitute was a bad thing, and that I'd be in danger if I was one."

"Oh, I see," the musician said, then laughed heartily, "So she really is a prude after all!"

"Wh-what do you mean?" the gobliness said.

"I always suspected it, to be honest. Why else would she be so insistent on the dancers changing back to their regular clothes so quickly after shows?" Bellows said, continuing to chuckle, "No, you're fine, she's just one of those people who doesn't like to think about sex is all. Probably finds it 'inappropriate' for some reason."

"But...isn't that how everyone is born?" Sheela said, confusion stepping into the place left behind by her draining sadness.

"Exactly my point!" the dwarfess said, gesturing with both hands in an exaggerated manner, "Makes no sense to me. It's an essential part of life, so why be ashamed of it! Especially odd, given some of the stuff dancers are known for. Maybe she's trying to fight that reputation? Anyway, prostitutes are just another kind of entertainer, so demeaning them is kind of the pot calling the kettle black."

"Yeah," the gobliness said after a few seconds of contemplation, "Yeah, you're right." She sat up a little taller.

"Now, that doesn't mean it isn't dangerous," Bellows said, "But life's dangerous, you know? Doing any job, you're sure to eventually piss someone off anyway, so why not do what you love?"

"Yeah," Sheela said, nodding, then turned to look at her companion, a more fresh look upon her face, "Um, one other thing. When I was out walking around town, I got to talking with someone who said becoming a new person might be a good way to get away from a past I don't like. Do you think that's okay? I don't know if I could really change my name…"

"Oh, Sheela," the dwarfess said, moving her hand up to the other small woman's shoulder, "Do you really think 'Bellows' is the name my parents gave me?"

The gobliness opened and closed her mouth a few times, then decided to remain silent.

"Of course that sort of thing is fine. Sometimes it's the only way for someone to survive, even," the musician said, "Besides, even those of us without a nasty past usually take a 'stage name'. It's part of the vanity of being a performer, I think. I will say this, though: it's important not to forget where you came from, even if you never admit it to anyone else. That way, you won't make the same mistakes twice."

"Thanks," Sheela said after a moment of contemplation, "That helps a lot."

She stood up and patted dust off of her skirt. Bellows finished brushing her beard, then started rebraiding it. Without the bonfire to blot them out, the stars captured Sheela's attention anew. The open sky still amazed the young woman, and the shapes that her mind's eye saw in the the stars reminded her of the runes she had etched upon her own flesh. Already, their inspiration was helping her to concoct new ideas for spells that would one day grace her form.

"I think I'll keep being me for now," the gobliness said, still staring upward, "But who knows? I might take a new name just so I can be more 'me' than I already am. Maybe that's what needs to happen."

"That sounds good," Bellows said, collecting her accordion, "Well, just let me know what to call you before the next show, in case I have to announce you." She winked at the other little lady, then headed off.

Sheela made her way back to Nora's wagon. Though they still burned, the torches were waning as they ran out of fuel. The calm of night rested upon the caravan, but Sheela's expectation of and hope for sleep would be delayed a little longer. Upon reaching her destination, she found Gerhard and Nora arguing. The little lady stayed outside, not wanting to interrupt them, but unable to prevent herself from listening in.

"I just don't understand why you have such a problem with it," Gerhard said emphatically, "It's a good plan."

"But why do you have to use her like that?" Nora said, "It's so...vulgar."

"Oh please," he said, "When I met you, you were-" The caravan leader's voice cut off abruptly.

Even without seeing them, Sheela could recognize the silence caused by a poorly timed remark.

"Because nobody will pay attention to her, especially if they think she's a courtesan" Gerhard said, trying a different tack, "If we're going to get screwed over again, I'd like to know enough to be able to come back at them. We won't get a better chance than having someone observant like Sheela right under their noses. Little thing gets into places before anyone realizes she's even nearby."

With a slightly smug expression, the gobliness used the man's words as her cue to enter the wagon silently. The exasperated man threw his hands up.

"Case in point," he said, then turned to Sheela with a sigh, "How much did you overhear? I don't want to have to repeat everything."

"Oh, not too long," she said, hands behind her back, a mock expression of innocence followed by a keen grin, "All I heard was that the plan is a good one, and that you want me to pretend to be a 'courtesan'. I'll need someone to explain what that is first, though."

"A courtesan is just a high-priced prostitute, Sheela," Nora said, interjecting before Gerhard had the chance to respond, "Nobody should have to subject themselves to that kind of experience, even for a little while."

"I appreciate that you're trying to protect me," Sheela said, walking over and trying to soothe the gypsy woman, "and you're right, nobody should be forced to do something like that. I know that better than you ever will. But this time, I want to. It's on my terms, after all, right?"

She looked to Gerhard, who nodded in agreement.

"So, what's so bad about that?" she said.

"Dancing is one thing," Nora said, shaking her head, "But that's just going too far in my opinion. It's not something good people do."

Sheela's expression soured, though she attempted to mask it. Lips closed, she ran her tongue over the sharp points of her teeth, carefully contemplating what to say next.

"If that's how it is, I guess I'm not good people," she said, then turned her attention to Gerhard, "So, tell me the rest of the plan."

"Good, I'm glad you're on board," he said, wringing his hands greedily, "There's a somewhat wealthy weapons merchant here in town. We're going to try to sell that sword we picked up to him, but I don't think he's going to give us a fair deal, so I'm going to bring you and Fenian along with me to check things out, just in case we need to come back."

"Okay," she said, "is there anything we should expecting to go wrong?"

"Well, I doubt he'll let servants into the office he'll use to talk money, so you'll probably be expected to wait out in the shop area," Gerhard said, "Fenian should be a good distraction for any guards on post, which would allow you to explore a bit. We'd be looking for where he'd hide money, storage for special products, things like that. But we're not taking anything, just making sure we know where it is."

"Sounds like a solid plan," Sheela said, "When's it going to happen?"

"Tomorrow," the gypsy man said, "So rest up. I'll come find you when we're ready to head out."

Nora stood up with a disgruntled sound and headed out the door. Sheela cocked an eyebrow, then gave Gerhard a questioning look.

"She does her best to act with 'decorum'," he said, shrugging, "I guess it's her way of distancing herself from a bad past; act like the nobles do in public, and maybe she'll become a proper lady or something. Shame she never bothered to find out what those people do in private. My nights would be much less cold." The caravan leader stared at the door in longing.

Sheela furrowed her brow, her mind whirling with the possibilities opened up for Nora's past, and followed the gypsy out in the hopes that the situation might be repaired somehow. The other woman had long since gone, so the gobliness headed back to the wagon they shared.

Inside, Nora was already sullenly bundled up in her small bed. Sheela considered saying something to her, but chose discretion as the better part of valor, and hoped her benefactor would feel less negative in the morning. The little lady dropped her new rucksack in the corner of the space she had been granted, and moved her bundle of material into it.

'There,' she thought, 'now it's in a place that's mine. Safe enough for now.'

Sheela gathered up the lap blanket and seat cushion that formed her bedding, and got as comfortable as she could. Though her mind raced with everything she had learned over the course of the day, her trek through the city quickly took its toll, and she drifted off into a dreamless sleep.

XI

Refreshed by a combination of rest and excitement, Sheela awoke the next morning without any prompting. She dressed in her dancer outfit, since it was the most appropriate set of clothes she had for the archetype in her mind, then did her best to wait patiently. The gobliness decided against working on her next rune, since the charcoal she would have to draw the designs with would make a mess, and decided to practice dancing instead.

Humming out a basic rhythm, she swung her hips side to side, creating an image akin to a ringing bell with the way she moved. She isolated her torso, holding it as still as she could manage, and tried various arm movements. Nothing felt quite right, so she changed from a stationary movement to a walking one. Continuing to swing, she bounced along the length of the wagon, and her arms naturally began to hit graceful balance points. The gobliness tried out this bounce-step several times, going back and forth. Each time, she refined the movements a bit more until she was satisfied with how it felt.

After taking a moment to breath, Sheela realized how odd it was that Nora had not woken her. She cracked open the door at the rear of the wagon to check outside, and found the sandy-haired gypsy working at a large pot over a fire. Performers filed past, bowls in hand, and she ladled up stew for each one. It was obvious from some of their faces that they had had too much fun the previous evening, but their expressions grew more pained as they got closer to Nora. However, the woman said nothing, much to the relief of everyone.

'Uh oh,' Sheela thought, closing the door quietly, 'how angry did I make her?'

The gobliness decided not to wait anymore, went out the side door of the wagon, and headed for Gerhard's cart. The early morning air felt muggier in the city than in the countryside, but still carried the chill of night, leaving her with a clammy sensation that caused the little lady to readjust her top to leave less skin exposed. Spotting a familiar, particularly well-dressed elf, she decided to try her new dance step out on him.

"Hey there, handsome," Sheela said, an inviting, yet predatory grin on her face as she bounced up, "Ready to be distracting?"

"Well, I can tell you are," Fenian said with a laugh. His face slowly grew more serious. "Did Gerhard explain why he wanted us to go in particular, though?"

"He said your job was to get any guards' attention while I looked for stuff," she said.

"Well, that's what we'll actually be doing, but there's other stuff, too," he said, "Elfs are assumed to be very high class, so if I play the servant, people will assume Gerhard is very high class, too."

"What about me?" the little lady said, raising an eyebrow.

"Well…" the elfen acrobat said, "How do I explain this nicely? You're a rarity. Most people have never even seen a female goblin."

"Right," Sheela said, having trouble making a connection, "We're usually kept in the home, so that's not surprising."

"Yeah," Fenian said, visibly struggling with what to say, "Having someone like that as a 'personal attendant' suggests that the things he has to sell are quite valuable."

The gobliness opened her mouth just slightly, and ran her tongue over the tips of her teeth as she thought. Anger flashed in her eyes, but was quickly overcome by annoyed comprehension.

"So everyone will just see me as another thing to be sold, then," she said after a moment.

"That's about the long and short of it, yes," he said.

"Well, at least that will make it easier for me to go unnoticed," Sheela said, a bitter twist now upon her lips.

"There's one other thing…" Fenian said, a touch of fear in his voice.

"Of course there is," the little lady said, running her fingers through her hair out of exasperation.

"Most elfs don't exactly have a good opinion of goblins," he said, "So once we're outside the camp, you can't act so familiar with me. I might even have to say some hurtful things to keep the image up."

"…but you don't actually have a problem with me?" she said. Her general anger with the world threatened to find a specific target.

"Of course not!" the elfen acrobat said, "But it would raise too many questions if we look too chummy. We have to appear to be just tolerating each other. That also makes Gerhard look more powerful, since he looks like he's keeping control of a situation that usually results in bloodshed."

Sheela huffed and crossed her arms. It was a good enough explanation that he had managed to avoid her disdain, but that did not mean she had to be happy about it.

"That's why I was so surprised when you knew my language," Fenian said, "I didn't expect that your clan would have done business with my kind."

"Well, it certainly explains why they always had a human there speaking for them," Sheela said, "I always assumed they just needed a translator, but I guess they just didn't want to get too close to the 'toads'."

"Ah," the elf said, his face a bit sullen, "You figured that word out, eh?"

"Yeah, like I said, I'm good with languages," the gobliness said, arms still folded, "I never thought much of us being called 'koakes', but it makes sense. We're just green, little, ugly swamp things, after all. Not the kind of people so refined a race as the elfs would deal with directly if they could avoid it."

A moment of silent tension settled upon the two like a sudden thick fog, blown away only by the door to Gerhard's wagon opening, and the caravan leader emerging. Fenian breathed a sigh of relief. Sheela merely turned her steely gaze upon the human man.

"Ah, you're both here already," Gerhard said, doing up a shirt that looked nice enough for a show, "We can head out early, then." He looked back and forth between the two a few times.

"Something wrong?" he said.

"No," Sheela said, jumping in before Fenian could. She took a breath before continuing. "No, nothing's wrong, we're ready to go." The gobliness shot a sideways glance toward the elf to tell him that they would continue their discussion later.

"Good!" the caravan leader said, handing the package containing the sword to Fenian, "Let's get going, then!"

The group took up a natural formation with Gerhard at the front and other two trailing slightly behind, with Sheela to the left and Fenian to the right. Even in the early morning, the crowds of Mirfield were relatively dense, if more muted than those of the midday market. As the three of them moved, people seemed to naturally get out of the way of the wedge they formed, giving the important-looking group space.

'I'll give you something to look at,' Sheela thought when she noticed Fenian lagging slightly behind out of the corner of her eye. She swayed her hips a little more, enjoying the fact that he could look, but did not dare touch in the current situation. The elf cleared his throat and tried to look like he had not noticed, then moved a little faster to get back to his position.

'Mmhm, that's what I thought.'

Rounding the corner, the trio saw that the shop they were headed for did, indeed, have guards. Two burly, poorly-shaved men stood in front of a doorway, a sign hung above their heads that simply said "Thorne's". The pair openly gave the group a visual dressing-down as they entered.

"G'morning!" a growling voice said from behind the counter. Though the man was too tall to be a dwarf, it was only just. His body seemed even smaller due to his rumpled, poorly tailored suit.

"Might I presume you are Mister Thorne?" Gerhard said.

Sheela continued to look about nonchalantly. Two more guards lurked near the corners by the shop's counter, but she could not see the reason why. All of the products on display appeared at first glance to be run-of-the-mill.

'Maybe they're here to prevent fights?' she thought.

"Yes, yes, I'm Thorne," the shop's owner said. His voice was too gravelly for such a small person. "Are you here to make a purchase or put something up for consignment?"

"Sell outright, actually," Gerhard said.

"That'll reduce the amount I can give you," Thorne said, a hard look in his eyes "Considerably."

"I'm willing to accept that," the caravan leader said, then snapped his fingers without breaking eye contact.

Fenian stepped forward and unslung the package, then handed it to Gerhard. Each of the guards shifted almost imperceptibly, their eyes on the elf and human. Ignored, Sheela continued to take in information.

As Gerhard unwrapped the box, the two men's hands tensed, ready to act if need be. The caravan leader then set the box down upon the counter and opened it, revealing the jeweled sword in all its glory. Thorne looked it over and nodded.

"A 'family heirloom', I assume?" the weasley merchant said, a hint of implication in his tone.

"Of course," Gerhard said with a straight face, "Had it for generations."

"Alright, let's step into the back, so I can inspect this a little closer," Thorne said. His guards relaxed once more. "Your servants will, of course, stay here. Too little space in the back, you understand."

"Of course," Gerhard said, putting on a face of disappointment as if he had not expected this to happen.

Thorne lead the way, ensuring that the door to the other room was open only long enough for the two of them to make it through. Left in the room alone together, there was a moment of awkward silence and shifting between Fenian, Sheela, and the guards before the elf spoke up.

"So, is this all you do for work," Fenian said after clearing his throat, "or do you have to pick up something else to make ends meet?" He was greeted with stone faced silence.

Though the men did not have the look of intelligence about them, they studied him in the way that a street dog studies a rat. Sheela took the opportunity to begin exploring the shop. The room in which they stood seemed off somehow, and she quickly came to the conclusion that outside of the building had been far too large for it and the office to be the only spaces available to Thorne.

'Must be a whole warehouse past there,' she thought as her eyes trailed past another door, this one somewhat hidden behind merchandise, to instead look at the variety of arms on display. In the back of her mind, she could hear Fenian continuing to chat at the guards.

Axes, daggers, maces, shields, and swords of all kinds made up the vast majority of the goods Sheela could see, but upon closer inspection, there were more interesting pieces mixed into the standard fare as well. A crescent-shaped blade hung among the axes, its edge on the inside of the curve, with an inward-facing hook that suggested attempting to run away might simply be a different way to die once the user of the weapon had you. A few columns over, strange daggers that went off at right angles from their hilts hung in a pair. Their shape reminded the gobliness of a farming implement she had seen in the fields they passed, only much smaller scale.

One mace's head was made up of only a heavy-looking wrought iron frame attached to a steel haft. Within it was a ball of cheap cotton skewered on a spike of the same iron. Unable glean its use, but uncomfortable with thinking on it too long, Sheela's attention slipped onward. The shields came in a number of shapes and sizes, but one in particular was of interest. Its surface was polished to such a highly reflective finish that she had initially mistaken it for a rounded mirror. Etched around its edge, the image of a snake wrapped around the protective piece's circumference.

Catching a familiar glint, however, her attention was immediately torn away. A blade edged with black, glass-like stone hung vertically by its metal hilt so as to prevent damage. The sword was shorter and narrower than the others around it, and its grip was smaller. Sheela recognized the symbols chiseled into its steel core, but could not read them.

'Must have been made by dwarfs,' she thought. Though their races shared an alphabet, the two languages were structured just differently enough that the script was functionally illegible to her.

Her eyes slid back to the blade's edge. The obsidian set in the metal formed the sword's actual cutting surface. She thought back to the flakes of black stone she had gotten to handle on occasion in the mines, only having ever found small pieces. The little lady stood in awe of the fact that, somewhere, there was enough of the stuff to make a whole weapon from it, even if the stone's fragility meant it needed to be set in a steel structure to hold its shape. Her hands automatically touched the runes that encircled her hips, remembering how the material's sharpness had helped her capture magic within her body.

"What're you doing there?" the angry voice of a guard said, dragging the gobliness back to the present.

"Hm, what?" Sheela said, blinking a few times. Her eyes stung, and she realized she must have been staring for quite some time. "Sorry, this one just reminded me of something is all." She started to reach out to indicate the obsidian-edged blade.

"No touching the merchandise," the guard barked, hand upon the hilt of his own sword.

"I was just point-" Sheela said, feeling wronged.

"Behave, little whore," Fenian said with a smug air, "Just because the master likes you doesn't mean you have free reign." However, his attitude changed quickly.

The look in the gobliness' eyes made the elf blanche. Even the guards edged back slightly, unsure of what fury the little woman would unleash. For a moment, the air around Sheela seemed to sizzle a golden color, but she took a deep breath, and the light around her melted away. The little lady's arms shook from how tightly her fists balled up, but she forced them open and shut several times, trying to get rid of the extra energy therein.

"Well then," Sheela said, her eyes locked on Fenian's, "if that's how you feel, don't expect me to ever service you again." There was a small amount of blood on the woman's sharp teeth from biting her tongue in her effort to remain calm.

Fenian coughed hard in a poor attempt to distract the guards from what Sheela had said, but was instead saved by Gerhard's emergence from the back room. He still carried the package containing the sword, and wore a vexed expression which only grew more irate when he saw the scene playing out.

"Come along, you two," the caravan leader said in a tone that left no room for argument, "We have business elsewhere."

"What about the other thing?" Thorne said, gesturing toward Sheela, "I'll still buy the little wench for fifty gold."

"For a night, maybe!" Gerhard said, then continued to walk after receiving no immediate answer, "We're leaving." His retinue followed quickly, not wanting to be left in a possibly dangerous situation.

Now more crowded, the people on the streets did not give way as easily, forcing the elf and gobliness to merely try and keep up with the human. A few blocks away, Gerhard stopped long enough to hand the sword package back to Fenian, then continued moving at a rushed pace, forcing Sheela to lift her skirts and practically run. She was still peeved, but got the distinct feeling that it was not yet time to air grievances. The elf, on the other hand, seemed more comfortable asking questions.

"So what happened back there?" Fenian said.

"The sword's a fake," Gerhard said without slowing or turning to look at them, "The jewels are glass and the gold is gilded on so thinly, you can scratch it off. If I ever meet the asshole who gave it to the villagers, I don't know if I'll punch him in the face or buy him a drink for pulling such a great con."

"How do you mean?" the acrobat said.

"Well, he probably hired some orcs to menace the town for a bit, then swooped in and 'saved' them all," the caravan leader said, shrugging, "Then gave them the sword in exchange for supplies worth far more than its value, and made off like a bandit."

The group moved in silence for a bit, making their way back toward the caravan. When they reached it, Gerhard made a direct line for his wagon, and nearly left the other two outside of it without a word. He hesitated at the door, and though his back was still turned, they could tell by the telltale 'scritch' of a match and the thin line of smoke that he had just lit a cigarette.

"Meet me here again tonight," he said, "Be ready to make some more money." The caravan leader then went into his wagon without another word.

"Well, he's certainly in a mood," Fenian said quietly a few seconds after the door shut.

"Yeah, and so am I," Sheela said, kicking the elf in one of his shins.

"Ah! What was that for?" he said, jumping at the impact.

"Do not. Ever. Call me a whore," the gobliness said, her eyes narrow slits as she growled the words through her teeth.

"But, I thought you were trying to become one!" Fenian said, confusion mixing with the pain on his face.

"No, I want to be a prostitute," Sheela said emphatically.

"They literally mean the same thing!" the acrobat said, his volume growing.

"Not to me they don't!" the little lady said, "One is a profession that I'd be damn good at, the other is what my father called me right before-"

There was practically an audible sound of suction as Sheela clammed up. Silence snapped into the conversation like a blast of cold air, and Fenian swallowed hard before continuing to speak. His words came out with a shocking amount of formality.

"...I see," he said, "I did not realize. My comment was entirely inappropriate, and I apologize."

The icy atmosphere pressed back in on the pair, though Sheela was beginning to wish that she had not been so volatile.

"Yes, well," she said, "Let's just both go get ready for tonight."

"I think that would be for the best," Fenian said, his face still blank.

They went their separate ways without another word. When Sheela got back to Nora's wagon, the gypsy woman was cleaning the area of the refuse left by people coming and going throughout the day.

"Hiya," Sheela said, "How's your day gone?"

"Hello," Nora said, not bothering to look in her direction, "If you want some food, there's cold stew in the pot on the stove. Feel free to get it yourself."

The disappointment in the woman's voice pierced the gobliness deeper than her anger ever had. Sheela nodded and climbed up into the wagon, unmotivated to try to get any more meaningful interaction out of her perturbed benefactor. She found the congealing pot of stew, ladled some into a bowl, and plopped down upon the stool she used to reach its high location to eat. However, even the copious meat the gobliness had dug through the pot for seemed flavorless due to the day's events.

'I really shouldn't have snapped like that,' Sheela thought, chewing a piece of fat, 'He didn't know.' She stared out the window at nothing in particular while she continued to eat. Eventually, Nora crossed her field of view and brought forth another conscious thought.

'And she's just trying to protect me,' the little lady thought, 'I mean, would Gerhard have really sold me if the price had been better?' The question lingered in her mind for an uncomfortably long period.

For the first time since that night around the fire, she felt unsafe. Though the caravan had become familiar, she realized that there was still much to learn about both its workings and those of the world around her. Despite leaving the mines behind, she had merely exchanged one ever-present danger for another.

'Still,' she thought, trying to convince herself, 'someone using me is better than guaranteed death, I suppose.'

The petulant, dissenting voice in the back of her mind told her it was not.

As she finished her meal, the gobliness slipped off of the stool. She set her bowl aside and found the paper and stick of charcoal. Drawing had always calmed her nerves, even if she had never been any good at it. However, the act also served to help her figure out new runes for spells she had in mind. One she had been toying with finally seemed right, so she tore its section of paper from the rest.

Getting to her feet, she held the piece with both hands and concentrated, closed her eyes and exhaled. A thin strand of gold radiance emerged from the place on her bosom just over her heart, twisted around her arm, and entered the paper. The rune upon it seemed to refine itself, going from smudged charcoal to fine calligraphy, and glowed with the light of the magic that infused it. Sheela opened her eyes, took a deep breath, and examined her work.

"Looks stable enough," she said, "Now let's see how effective it is."

Sheela crumpled the paper in one tiny fist. There was a burst of energy, and flakes of paper dissolved into the air between her fingers. The air around the hand wavered slightly, then turned orange as the flame engulfed it. With a bit of concentration, she was able to push the fire's temperature high enough to turn it blue, then pull it back down to being a mere shimmer on the air.

"I guess I'll be able to do it on purpose now…" Sheela said wistfully, thinking back to the final night in the mines.

When she stopped thinking about it, the flame returned to its neutral orange. She opened her fingers and turned her hand over several times, marvelling at the fact that the fire did not spread past her wrist. Taking another deep breath, she let the magic fade. Where the blaze had been, she was happy to see that her soft skin was untouched.

'Not enough time to add it to my belt right now,' she thought, her other hand unconsciously rubbing the line of runes embedded around her hips, 'Guess I'd better just draw some more.'

Sitting back down, Sheela spent about an hour drawing the symbol over and over again until she felt she had reproduced it well enough. The magic went in a little easier the second time. She smiled slightly, glad that the new spell was beginning to feel almost effortless. Large splotches of mulberry were beginning to show up in her eyes, and she bit her lip at the realization that, with the way she had left things with Fenian, she might not get a chance to recharge for some time.

"Can't worry about it now," she said aloud to herself, "Gotta' focus on the task at hand."

The light coming in through the windows was the dim orange of early evening. Sheela washed her hands, tucked the new scrap of paper with the extra rune on it into her brassier, then once more slipped out the side door, hoping to avoid Nora. However, the sandy-haired woman caught the gobliness momentarily in her gaze, then looked away, a crestfallen expression on her face. The little lady considered saying something to her, asking what had happened in the gypsy's life to cause such distress, but found herself unable to do so. Instead, she merely sulked away as she went to meet Fenian and Gerhard.

XII

Around Sheela, the people of the caravan were packing up their wagons. Though she had enjoyed her time in Mirfield, the gobliness understood that if things went badly, they would have to leave quickly. What surprised her, though, was that some wagons were already beginning to head out. The two people she had been expecting, Fen and Gerhard, were already outside the caravan leader's wagon when she got there. Curiously, though, Lebar was also present, sitting in the driver's seat.

"Hey everybody," Sheela said, "Having the big guy take your wagon out for you?"

"Yes, indeed," Gerhard said, "We were just waiting to see if you would show up."

"Ah," she said, feeling guilty, "Fen told you about what happened."

"My door isn't that thick, little one, and you were standing just outside it," he said, "Fenian didn't have to tell me anything."

Sheela looked at the ground and shuffled her feet a bit. Fenian was trying equally hard not to look uncomfortable.

"None of my business as long as it doesn't interfere with what we need to do," Gerhard said, then turned to the half-giant, "Go on, Lebar, you know where we'll meet up."

The massive man nodded his head, then cracked the reins. The wagon creaked and strained forward, leaving dust in its wake as it picked up speed.

"So, Sheela, when we were there earlier, did you have time to check out what might be worth something?" Gerhard asked, watching the wagon go.

"There were a few things in the shop," she said, "But I think we'll find better stuff elsewhere in the building. There's probably a storage room in the back for the really good pieces."

"Anything in particular that caught your eye, though?" he said, his eyes shifting sideways to look at her.

"Well," she said, thinking back, "there was a sword with a black stone edge. That looked really expensive."

"Alright," Gerhard said, "So here's the plan: I'd prefer to just sneak in completely unnoticed, but it's likely we'll have to get past guards. Sheela, I trust you can get their attention while we do that?"

"Yeah, shouldn't be a problem," the gobliness said confidently.

"Okay," the caravan leader said, then turned to the lithe elf, "Once they're out of the way, Fenian, you and I will make our way into the building and grab everything valuable we can."

"What about the guards inside?" the acrobat said. Gerhard looked back to the gobliness.

"I'll see what I can do," Sheela said with a slight shrug.

"You'll think of something, I'm sure," the caravan leader said with a sly smile.

As the group headed back into town, they did not make themselves as known as they had in the daylight. Though Sheela had not changed her garb, the other two wore more muted colors. The gobliness wondered if she, too, should have gone for something more subtle, but remembered that she was to be the distraction.

'No better distraction in the world,' she thought hiking up her barely contained bosom, 'If what I've been able to do in the past holds true, a few guards'll be no problem.'

With Fenian and Gerhard there, Sheela noticed that the bedraggled people she had seen the previous night kept a much greater distance. At first, it was a relief, but when she caught sight of one of the people's face's, she realized it was because they were afraid of the group. Pushing the implications of this to the back of her mind, the gobliness concentrated instead on keeping up with the elf and human men.

Moving at a good clip, they reached Thorne's shop a few minutes later. Two guards still stood outside, but they were a different set of men from those they had met earlier.

"Night watch," Gerhard said quietly, peeking around the corner of the street, "We got lucky. They won't know our faces." He looked at Sheela and jerked his head in the direction of the guards.

As she strode forth into the pool of light around the shop's entrance, the gobliness began to swing her hips once again. The show was just as much to taunt Fenian as it was to grab the attention of the two men in front of the building. Their mix of tension and confusion at her approach was exactly the result the little lady had been looking for.

"Good evening, gentlemen," Sheela said, her hands on her hips as she looked up at them, "How's the night treating you?"

One guard, the younger of the two, nervously put a hand on his sword, then looked to the other man for an indication of what he should do next. The older guard held his ground and shot a stern look down at the gobliness. Her shark-toothed smile returned as she decided on her target.

"Move along," the older guard said, "No business for you here. We're on duty."

"Aw," Sheela said, batting her eyelashes, "But it's so cold out here. I'm sure we could all do with finding someplace nice and warm. I know I'm absolutely chilled to the bone."

She placed a hand to her chest and stroked it in a slow downward motion. This stimulation caused bumps to appear in the fabric of her brassier, giving the distinct impression that she was, indeed, quite cold. Her other hand subtly made it to the older guard's thigh and, locking eyes with the man to hold his attention, there was a nearly imperceptible glow where she touched him.

Clearing his throat a second later, the guard's disposition shifted as he blinked repeatedly. As her smile crept slowly back across her lips, Sheela squeezed his leg meaningfully. A look of internal conflict flashed across the man's face, but then his eyes returned to a neutral expression.

"Uh, yes, well," he said, clearing his throat again, "Perhaps spending some time in front of a hearth would be a good idea."

"Didn't you say we weren't to-" the younger man said.

The First Night

"It's a quiet night, boy!" the guard in control said fervently, then continued more calmly, "I'm sure it would be fine for us to go relax, if only for a few moments."

The younger companion looked nervously back and forth between the more experienced guard and the gobliness. He gawped and stammered, searching for something to say.

"Come this way," the older man said to Sheela, ignoring the protestations of his inferior, "We have a side room for meals and such." He lead her into a narrow alley between the building and its neighbor. The younger guard held his ground for a moment more, but acquiesced when it became clear he was going to be left alone otherwise.

Using a narrow door, they entered a small room with no decoration other than a small wooden table and a few stools. The fireplace in the room was tiny, and its masonry was different from that of the rest of the wall, suggesting that it had been added at a later date instead of during construction. Despite this, it still provided enough heat to fill the diminutive space with a pleasant warmth.

The younger guard rushed past Sheela and the older man to shut a door on the other side of the room. Before her did so, however, the gobliness saw rows of shelving filled with boxes of various shapes and sizes.

'So there is more storage back here,' Sheela thought, 'I wonder how many more guards there are…'

"Well, since you were nice enough to bring me inside, I should do something for you in return," she said, a suggestive lilt in her voice, "Is there anyone else who could come enjoy the show?"

"See if you can find the other two, Rodney," the older guard said. Sweat was beginning to gather on his temples, as if he were straining himself.

"But, Tomas…" the younger guard, Rodney, said.

Tomas shot his subordinate a glance that confirmed it was an order, causing Rodney to shoot out into the storage area like a pursued villain.

'Hope he doesn't take too long,' Sheela thought, watching him go.

"By the by," Tomas said, "You wouldn't happen to be a, uh, seamstress, would you?"

"Well, I don't work at that shop downtown, if that's what you're asking," the little lady said, slowly facing the burly man once more, "But I would like to apply there. Think I need some practice to make sure I do well? Maybe I could loosen your trousers for you? They look a little tight."

Her hand returned to the man's thigh, but glided further up before pressing into it. However, as he was opening his mouth to speak, Rodney came back in with another man. Tomas cleared his throat loudly again, and reached down to pick the gobliness up.

"Here, let me help," he said, easily lifting her onto the table. His grip was firm, and it seemed to linger a moment around her waist, as if he did not want to let go. "This way, everyone can see you dance. You do dance, don't you?" He quickly took a seat to mask the tent he had pitched in his trousers.

"Of course I do," Sheela said, bouncing her hips to each side, then donned a confused expression, "But I thought you were going to get two more...?" Her gaze fell upon Rodney, and the younger man finally fell to her charms, even without the lubrication of magic.

"I could only find Syd," he said, his prominent adam's apple bobbing, "I- I could go look again."

"No, that's fine," she said, shifting her weight to her other leg, and crossing her arms under her bust, "Fewer people will make it more intimate."

'I hope Fen and Gerhard can deal with the last one, then,' Sheela thought.

The First Night

Both Rodney and the new man joined Tomas silently at the table. Sheela took a deep breath, and exhaled slowly. There was a slight shimmer of gold, and the sound of escaping air grew. It first became a low hum, then evolved into a steady beat akin to drums made of leather and wood. The gobliness shook her hips repeatedly, and the unmistakeable sound of coins clinking against one another filled the air.

As she moved, her arms rose into the air and her right leg extended forward, then curled to the left. She spun around to give the men a full look at her body, and stopped side-on to Tomas, locking eyes with the man. A front to back motion began in the gobliness' hips and travelled upward, exaggerating every curve of her body along the way. She turn her eyes upon the two subordinate guards, who she was facing, and repeated the same motion side-to-side with an added forward pop to her chest.

Satin and taffeta swished as Sheela lifted her skirt slightly to expose more leg. Though the gobliness had a bit of pudge to her overall, her calf muscles bunched powerfully each time she pointed her feet. The little lady kicked at the fabric behind her, then out to the front once more, and threw her head back as she stamped down to the rhythm of the ethereal drums. As her head snapped upright, her bright red hair splayed out around her, then crept forward around her face. Though this might have made her look shy and reserved, the aggressive countenance she wore instead made her appear as hunting cat among the tall grass.

Each man present became fully enthralled as Sheela continued to dance. Due to the combination between her sensual style and the cultural taboos surrounding her race, the gobliness was an exotic treat that none of them had been prepared for. As her arms flowed and her hips rolled, however, the little lady's mind was elsewhere. She concentrated on maintaining the music as long as her magic would last to cover any noise that might be happening outside the room, and allowed her years of training to move her body automatically.

When Tomas' grabbed her once more, it caught Sheela by surprise, and her concentration broke. The music ceased in an instant, and she blinked repeatedly, as if waking from a fitful sleep. Her eyes shown in the torchlight, not a fleck of gold remaining within them from the effort of sustaining the music as long as she had.

"Oh my," Sheela said, still attempting to play coy, despite her irritation, "I didn't realize my dancing had become so good!"

"Yes, little goblin, you move very well!" Tomas said. His grip was more firm than comfortable, and only tightened further at the sound of breaking glass from out in the warehouse.

"What was that?" Syd, the third guard, said, no longer distracted by the tiny dancer.

Without a thought, he ran back out into the room he was supposed to have been patrolling. Rodney decided to take his cues from the more motivated guard instead of the senior one, and followed closely behind, leaving Sheela and Tomas alone in the small room.

"So, you want to be a seamstress, eh?" he said, the crackling fire reflecting in his wild eyes, "How's about you show me what other skills you think qualify you for that kind of job?" The man breathed heavily, and the smell of sweat became more powerful as leaned closer to her.

'Shit, maybe that spell was more powerful than I realized,' Sheela thought, her mind racing as she realized it would be physically impossible for her to overpower him, 'That, or his mind is even weaker than most goblin men. Either way, I don't have time for this!' A half-formed plan struck her, and she decided it was better than nothing.

"I'd be glad to," she said, using both hands to push her hair back, "Just put me back on the ground, and I'll be at the perfect height to give you a demonstration." The gobliness licked her lips and thrust out her chest to drive the point home.

Tomas complied, once more lifting the little lady with ease, and deposited her on the ground in front of himself. Not wasting a moment, he loosed his pants, and dropped them around his ankles. What was revealed was much larger than Sheela was used to dealing with, but looked about the same size as Fenian's member had felt, so she was not really surprised. The little lady, did, however, play it up as if she had been.

"My goodness!" she said, her eyes wide, and one hand upon her chest, "I don't know if I can fit something so large!" She let her mouth hang open, as if in astonishment.

"Oh, I'm sure you'll find a way," Tomas said, a lecherous grin on his face as he reached out to grasp at her head.

"Now, now, I don't want to start before you're really ready," Sheela said, her hand shifting over, "Maybe you'd like to see a little more of me to get you there?"

She lifted one of her breasts out of its cup. It maintained its shape relatively well, even without the support of her brassier, and the exposed areola and nipple were dark evergreen against the yellow-green of the rest of her body. Tomas nodded needlessly, as the rising of his mast was more than enough to indicate he wanted her to keep going.

As Sheela reach into the other cup, she grabbed the scrap of paper tucked within. In one smooth motion, she crumpled the rune and thrust her blazing fist up into Tomas exposed nether regions. The senior guard howled at the impact, the sound evolving into a scream as the sensation of extreme heat set in afterward. He fell backward and curled up on the floor.

"I think the proper etiquette is to pay before you touch, no?" Sheela said. Tomas whined as another loud crash came from the warehouse. "Seems like your boys have their hands full, so I'll just let myself out."

Back outside, the gobliness followed the alley back toward the street she had come in from, and headed back around the corner from which they had first observed the guards. Taking a moment to catch her breath, she re-situated herself within her top, and looked around to see if anyone else had made it out. The sound of a window being smashed brought her attention back to Thorne's weapon shop.

Gerhard was rolling across the road, having jumped through the glass, and was followed shortly by Fenian leaping through the opening the other man had created. Sheela ran to them, and helped the elf lift the human to his feet. No words were necessary, as the caravan leader immediately began running, despite the fall he had taken and the heavy pack on his back. All the gobliness could do was try to keep up.

Behind them, angry sounds could just be made out as others came to investigate the noise, but the group pressed on without feverishly. At first, Sheela wondered why they were not bothering to use the side streets to hide, but thought back to the faces of those night-time citizens of Mirfield they had already encountered, and realized that she preferred even a straight shot in the open to entering the world of those trodden upon by society. She wondered if any who entered ever got out again.

Instead, the group bolted down the main road, heading for Mirfield's exit as fast as they possibly could on foot. As they passed the ancient, decaying barrier that had once protected the city from invasion, the tight formation of buildings began to spread out. A few hundred feet into the outer city, Lebar waited with Gerhard's wagon.

"Come on," he said, his booming voice a barely controlled whisper, "we haven't got all night!"

Gerhard stepped aside and opened the back door of the cart, allowing the running Fenian to vault into the vehicle. Sheela's eyes grew wide as she became aware of the fact that her momentum was carrying her unstoppably toward something that usually took her a careful few minutes to get up onto due to her height. As she braced for the impact against the stairs, her feet left the ground. The gobliness opened her eyes in time to ready herself for a different hit entirely, as she realized that the caravan leader had grabbed and flung her into the wagon before jumping aboard himself. As she flew across its interior and bounced across the floor, the little lady heard the elfen acrobat knocking on the front wall.

"We're all in," Fenian yelled, "Go! Go now!"

The wagon's axles groaned in time with Sheela as she stood up, rubbing her rump and checking to see if there was any serious damage from her flight and subsequent crash. The floor rocked and all of the props and tricks jostled on their hooks and in their cubbies as the group sped away from the town that had been so interesting. She sighed, wondering if she would ever get the chance to go back.

"Well, that was certainly an adventure," Gerhard said, his voice strangely chipper as he took off the overstuffed sack on his back.

"An adventure?" Sheela said in a perturbed tone, still looking herself over and trying to catch her breath, "Sheesh, I didn't realize your 'adventure' would hurt that much! I don't think I've ever run that fast in my life."

"Well, you looked good doing it," Fenian said, then shrunk a little at the gobliness' annoyed glance.

"Anyway, you two, we got a good haul, so let's have a look at it," Gerhard said.

As the caravan leader began to unpack his take, Fenian set down his own ruck and did the same. Sheela was left with nothing to do but run the events of the evening through her head. After a few moments of watching the two men sort, the thoughts forced their way out into the open.

"So, the big guy was pretty easy to take care of," she said, "though I didn't expect my spell to do more than get me inside. He must have already been thinking about boinking me beforehand."

"How'd you 'take care' of him?" Gerhard said, still sorting.

"Well, he got handsy and broke my concentration, which made my music spell fail," Sheela said, shrugging, "Then you two made all that noise, and the other two guards left to investigate it, so I gave him a handjob he'll never forget. What was all that ruckus, anyway?" She looked at Fenian, hoping for a reaction, but was disappointed when he did not seem to notice. Instead, Gerhard's reaction came as a complete surprise.

"Oof, not a good way to go," the caravan leader said.

"Mm, I suppose it wouldn't be," the gobliness said thoughtfully, "but I'm sure he'll get over it."

"He'll do what?" Gerhard said, his eyes narrow slits.

"I mean, it wasn't as easy for him as I made it sound," she said, unnerved by the sudden change of mood, "I'm pretty sure his burns are bad enough that he'll think again abo-"

"You didn't kill him?" Gerhard said. The rumble of the road seemed to fill an impossibly long moment before she answered.

"...No, why would I?" Sheela said. The air became ice, and she was taken back to the first night she had seen the group, when he had had a similar reaction. Now, she understood why everyone else had gone silent.

"You didn't…!" the human man said, his eyes growing wide and wild, "Why not? Now he'll tell his boss about you, and they'll connect it back to us!" He stood suddenly and looked as if he were about to lunge at the gobliness.

"Boss, what's done is done, right?" Fenian said, backing away from the infuriated caravan leader, "Not anything we can do about. An honest mistake, right?" He looked to the gobliness, who agreed weakly by nodding her head.

Gerhard swiveled his head around to the elf, breathing heavily, and stared at him for a terrifyingly long time. The two seemed to have an unspoken conversation before the caravan leader turned back to her, his eyes filled with simmering rage.

"We can never go back there, now," he said in an unnervingly calm voice, "If we do, Thorne will have us killed. No police, no law, we just disappear. Do you understand?"

Sheela nodded once more, slowly at first, but with growing intensity in each movement. Gerhard seemed to accept the situation, and went back to sorting the goods they had stolen, but the gobliness could not take her eyes off the man for fear that his temper might flare up once more.

The rest of the trip to rejoin the caravan was spent in silence. When they reached the new camp an hour later, Sheela silently disembarked. Though she did not know where Nora's wagon was, she had long since decided that wandering would be better than spending any more time under Gerhard's icy gaze. The gobliness did not realize she was being followed until a hand was on her shoulder.

"Hey," Fenian said, "Mind if I join you?" The elf had something wrapped in cloth in his other hand, but Sheela did not much care what it was at the time. Nor was his mistake earlier in the day important any longer. She was just glad to have someone to talk to.

"I didn't know I would be expected to kill anyone," she said, staring at the ground as she walked.

"Could you have done it if you had known?" she said, staring at the sky.

"I don't know," the little lady said, "Maybe? If I know someone deserved it, I wouldn't have any problem doing it, but those guys were just doing their jobs, you know?"

"You say that," the acrobat said, "But you never really know what you'll do until you're faced with the situation."

"Oh, I know I would do it," Sheela said darkly, "If they deserved it."

There was an emphasis to her voice that made Fenian stop and look at the gobliness. She looked up at him, a hard, sad look in her eyes.

"Wow," Fenian said as he connected the dots.

"They were going to sacrifice me, Fen," she said, "As a clan, they decided that any woman who thought for herself was worthy of punishment by death."

"All of them, they're all...?" he said.

"It was a pretty big fire, so I hope so," she said, and continued walking, her eyes cast once more downward. Again, she felt a hand touch her shoulder.

"Look, I know it might not be much, but you deserve this," the elf said, holding the long, cloth-covered object toward her, "In more ways than one, it sounds like."

Sheela took the bundle and began to unwrap it. She recognized the grip and hilt; it was the dwarfen sword from Thorne's shop. The gobliness sighed wearily, then laughed.

"I guess I do, don't I?" she said.

"A little sword, its edge forged in elemental fire," Fenian said, "If I had a more poetic mind, I'd say it was made for you."

Another bitter laugh escaped the little lady, and she looked up at the stars. They seemed more distant than they had on that first night, when she had run so hard and far from the consequences of her actions. Her vision blurred as tears began to roll down her face.

"There, there," he said as she buried her face in his leg, "Go ahead and let it out."

They stood in the middle of the camp, Sheela weeping openly as everything that had happened finally sank in. Fenian placed a hand on her head as some small comfort, but otherwise remained still. When the gobliness finally ran out of tears, she did her best to wipe her face, but just ended up playing with her long hair in an embarrassed manner.

"I must look a mess," she said, practically trying to hide among the tangle of her red locks.

"No, you look fine," Fenian said, ruffling her hair further, "Really beautiful for a goblin, actually."

"Watch it, mister," Sheela said. Though she had meant it to sound angry, her voice instead made it clear she did not really have the energy to fight.

"Oh, it's 'mister' now, is it?" he said, "Maybe I shouldn't invite you in, then, since we're still being so formal?"

As the gobliness looked around at the camp for the first time since they started walking, she realized that they were in front of the elf's small wagon. She chuckled to herself.

"I mean," she said, "You could ask me in. If you wanted to."

Despite putting a bit of effort into trying to seem coy, what the little lady said actually carried a genuine hope of not being alone for the evening. Beyond the fact that she was in an emotionally needy place, there was an itch at the back of her mind that let her know she was totally out of magic.

"Well, since I have your permission, then," Fenian said, opening the door in gentlemanly manner, "Would you like to come inside?"

"I would be glad to," Sheela said as she hopped up onto the stoop, then daintily lifted her skirt to match the elf's mock of high society.

A warm, dark sleeping space greeted the gobliness. As she had expected, it was barely wide enough for a reasonably sized bedroll. When the elf stepped in with a small lantern in hand, however, color seemed to take over the room. The unanticipated surprise was the result of hundreds of baubles and bangles hanging from the ceiling of the wagon. The various beads, feathers, and pieces of jewelry caught and reflected light and color about the wagon's interior, making the small space seem somehow larger.

"Trophies from previous conquests," Fenian said with a grin, "Care to contribute something?"

"Oh, is that all I am?" Sheela said, still trying to play innocent.

"Don't tell me you expected more," he said, laying down on his side, mock disappointment in his voice, "and after all of that bluster about me not trying to romance you?"

"I suppose not," she said, "After all, you're just a source of magic to me."

"Hmph," the elf said indignantly, "So I'm just a piece of meat, then?" He rolled onto his back, then turned his head away from her.

"That depends," the gobliness said, carefully straddling his thighs and leaning forward, "Does being in my mouth sound like fun?" She licked her lips hungrily.

"Heh, yes it does, indeed," Fenian said, then quickly added, "But no teeth, please."

"I make no promises," Sheela said, pulling back her lips and biting at the air with her shark-like fangs.

Making for the string lacing his trousers shut, the little lady's curiosity was peaked when the acrobat placed a hand on her shoulder. Looking up from her task, she saw his smug face and gently wagging finger.

"Not yet," he said, "You may be good at finishing things up, but there's a thing called foreplay, you know?"

"Had to go and make things complicated, didn't you?" she said, sticking her tongue out.

"I'm just looking out for you," Fenian said innocently, "After all, the longer you can keep a customer pleased, the more money you'll make. So, really, it's just a good habit to be in."

'Oh,' Sheela thought, 'I hadn't thought of that.'

With this in mind, the gobliness redirected her attention. Her hands moved up his torso, applying just enough pressure to untuck his shirt. She leaned back, then forward once more, infiltrating the garment. As she spread her fingers and ran then over his smooth skin, the elf smiled and closed his eyes.

Carefully watching his reactions, Sheela learned what places on Fenian were the most sensitive, and where she should not touch. Other than a couple of ticklish spots she filed away in her brain for possible later torture, she found what felt like a deep scar on his left side that caused his to wince, even on a mild touch.

"Did that hurt?" she said in a cooing voice.

"Like hell," he said, "A knife in the stomach usually does."

"I'm sure," the gobliness said, "but I meant does it still hurt when you touch it?"

"No," the elf said, his voice searching for how to continue, "Not physically, anyway. But memory has a funny way of not fading when you actually want it to."

"Mm," Sheela said, nodding sagely, "Given how tonight's adventure went, though, I'm surprised you didn't come out with any new injuries."

"Who said I didn't?" Fenian said, opening his eyes and grinning down at her, "I think you should probably inspect my body, just to make sure." He leaned up slightly and pulled his shirt the rest of the way off.

The scar on his belly was the only real blemish on the elf's otherwise pristine skin. However, as she studied him further, the gobliness noticed slight tan lines around his neck and upper arms. They were emphasised by the colorful light of the wagon, as was the greenish color of her own skin against the deep purple of her outfit.

"I don't know," she said, "I think I'd better have a closer look…"

Sheela leaned down and began to kiss his abdomen, starting just below his bellybutton, and ending around his collar bone. When she finished her upward crawl, she backed up a bit to find the right position, then pressed her pelvis against his. With no undergarments covering her, the rough leather of Fenian's trousers was instantly stimulating, but what excited the little lady more was the growing bulge she could feel trying to escape the confines of his clothes.

Sitting back up, the gobliness pressed her minute body weight downward against the elf's pelvis. Her hands trailed back across his stomach and up her own torso, hugging each curve along the way, and rose into the air. Grinding against him, Sheela began to move her hips in the same way she would if dancing for an audience. The direct contact caused both her and the acrobat between her legs to breath deeply and slowly in order to maintain control.

Just as the little lady was beginning to wonder if her actions were having any effect, Fenian's hands began to climb her thighs slowly. As his fingers passed her belt of runes, she felt the first tingle of magic returning, and smiled, redoubling her efforts. Bending her elbows and dropping her hands behind her head and neck, she easily found the knot holding her brassier together, then deftly took it apart. The gobliness dropped the garment beside herself, then leaned forward slightly, placing her hands on the elf's lower abdomen once more, and squeezing her freed breasts between her upper arms as a result.

It was not long before Fenian took them firmly in his hands, and Sheela smiled at both his reaction and the relief to her back. She had always been a chubby child, but when she bloomed into womanhood, it had come with some spectacular surprises that left all of the boys who had teased her instead seeking her attention in a much more positive way. However, her muscles had yet to fully catch up to her endowments, so she was glad for his support.

"I'd prefer to be on my back," she said, putting her hands over his as he continued to knead, "but I don't know if I want to give you that much control."

"Why would I wait for you to give it to me?" he said, a wily smirk spreading on his features.

His hands moved back to her hips, and his swiveled about, holding her as if she weighed nothing. Sheela suddenly found herself beneath Fenian, feeling even tinier than she normally did next to the elf. His body was haloed by the colorful light reflecting from the trophies he had hanging from the ceiling, and the small lines of muscle on his body were emphasized by the shadows. As the elf loosed his trousers, the gobliness' grin grew.

'I can handle that, right?' Sheela thought, the notion occurring to her for the first time as she gazed down at Fenian's manhood, 'Yeah, I'll be alright.'

As she reassured herself, however, her gaze moved up to his face. The eyes were not what she had expected. The half-crazed lust directed toward her that she had grown used to in most of her encounters was not present. Instead, they were filled with self-satisfaction. There was no time to contemplate the meaning of it, though, as all concerns were pushed to the back of the little lady's mind when he entered her.

Sheela squeezed her eyes shut and concentrated on relaxing. Pain presented itself to her senses, but the feeling of pressure from something so comparatively large being inside her small body was much more intense. Muscles began to twitch, and the gobliness had to actively think about breathing in order to not hold her breath.

"Doing okay down there?" Fenian said, a smug tone in his voice.

"Yeah," Sheela said, her voice airy, "Just feeling rather full at the moment."

"And I haven't even gotten all the way in," he said, slowly closing the gap between them, "Sure you can take it?"

"Oh, would you just do it alrea-" she said, her defiance cut off as he complied, "W-wow. Okay. See, I knew it'd fit." Despite her statement, the gobliness was seeing stars. It hurt, but also made her skin crawl in a pleasant way.

'I could get used to this,' she thought, 'Come to think of it, I guess just about everyone up here will be this big. Or bigger.' An image of the half-giant Lebar flashed across her mind, and she wondered if everything scaled up, or just his height. She quickly brushed the thought aside, however, and concentrated on the activity at hand.

Each time Fenian moved, Sheela's vision seemed to frost over. While she firmly believed it to be because of the difference in scale between the two of them, the gobliness also realized that she had not had such contact with another person in more than a month. Though she had always been sensitive, taking such a long time between intimate acts had heightened the experience. Her reflexes were still strong, though; the very moment she felt a spark of magic, the rune in her mouth flashed.

"What was that?" Fenian said, surprised.

"Just getting ready for when you blow," Sheela said, broadcasting a bit of smugness herself, "Remember my special spell?" She opened her mouth to display the symbol beneath her tongue, but also used the opportunity to lick her lips slowly.

"Ah yes," he said, continuing to move at a growing pace, "So if I want to just fill you up with my seed, you wouldn't mind?"

"Go ahead," she said, fighting to keep her mind grounded enough to speak, "I'll be safe, so if that's what you want, go for it."

As the elf's pace continued to increase, the gobliness' used her hands and arms to frame her ample chest and keep her breasts from bouncing too hard due to the rigorous movements. She found that, once she was accustomed to his size, she could still exert some control over how tight she was, and squeezed him at every pull. Fenian shuddered each time she did so.

"Keep that up, and it'll happen sooner than I expected," he said, and gritted his teeth.

"I'm ready whenever you are," Sheela said, reaching up with one hand, "So why not just let it happen?"

She touched his chest, brushing her fingertips over his skin, and felt the same goosebumps that crawled over her own.

Beside her head, the elf's fist bunched up the fabric of his thin mattress. The gobliness gave him one final squeeze as he thrust, then gasped for air as even more pressure welled within her. Her breath came in short, sharp bursts, and she threw her head back. Fluid quickly surrounded the already-large intrusion within her body, and began to leak out. The sensation of it tantalized her without the need for either of them to move.

For a beautiful moment, Sheela floated on a haze of colorful light. As her vision began to clear, it was filled with stars for a moment more when Fenian pulled out. She took a deep breath and ran her hands over her own skin. Nerves twanged happily as she passed over her erect nipples and across her belly. Pushing the waist of her skirt back down, she could see the soft, golden glow of the spells carved into her body, full of magic.

"That was fun," Fenian said, sitting up and breathing heavily. His head just barely brushed some of the longer trophies hanging from the ceiling.

"Mm," Sheela said, still enjoying her own body, "we should do that again sometime."

"We'll see," the elf said, his tone a touch distant.

"I'll have to see about giving you something for your collection later," the gobliness said, oblivious to the implication.

"Will you need help getting back to Nora's wagon?" he said.

Several attempts at sitting up later, Sheela tried to stand, only for her legs to immediately give beneath her.

"Yes," she said sheepishly, "Can you pass me my top?"

"Oh, I suppose," Fenian said, brushing the material of it past her sensitive skin as he handed it off.

"Thank you, kind sir," Sheela said, sticking her tongue out at him. She tied the garment back up and situated herself comfortably within its depths. As she finished doing so, the elf pulled her up onto his back. She happily wrapped her arms around his neck.

"Just try not to drip on me, alright?" he said, standing up. He grabbed her wrapped-up sword before heading out the door.

"That wouldn't be entirely my fault, y'know," she said, "Besides, I'm more worried about my skirt."

"Yeah, but leather's hard to clean," Fenian said.

"Should have thought about that before keeping your pants part-way on, then," Sheela said, pointing down at the elf's groin.

"Ah, damn it..." he said, causing her to laugh.

The rest of the walk back to Nora's wagon was completed in silence. Sheela spent most of it looking up at the sky. Though the fires and torches of the camp dampened the scene above slightly, it was still amazing to her. It was also comforting to be so close to Fenian, though she kept reminding herself that they shared no real connection, other than the physical. For the moment, however, she allowed herself to indulge in the possibility.

Though the journey home was shorter than she would have liked, it was enough for the exhausted gobliness to regain her legs. The elf placed her gently on the top step of the cart, then handed her the sword she had won for the evening's work.

"It was a good job tonight, even if you left a loose end," Fenian said.

"Was it?" Sheela said, still unsure due to Gerhard's reaction, "I'll take your word for it, I guess."

"We'll all be busy rehearsing until we reach Briar Glen," he said, "So I'll see you around."

"Yup," she said, "Have a good night."

"You too," the elf said.

As Fenian headed off into the night, Sheela made her way inside. Nora was already asleep, but tossed fitfully as the gobliness padded across the floor. After setting the sword flat on its side to protect its fragile edge, the little lady bundled up in her own small blanket, and promptly lay awake for hours. Though she had no context for the meaning of breaking up with somebody, she had an unshakable feeling that she had somehow lost something with the elf after that night.

XIII

The next week of travel was busy for Sheela, both mentally and physically. Her days were filled with dance rehearsals and chores, while her nights were spent trying to understand everything that had happened that evening in Mirfield. She hesitated to speak with Gerhard, in case he was still angry with her, but also found that Nora was continuing to act like a wall when asked about anything other than what she referred to as "respectable" work. Eventually, the gobliness broke down and spoke to Bellows about the incident.

"I don't want to know anymore about what happened with Thorne," the dwarfess said after a few moments, twiddling away at her accordion as they spoke.

"But would it really have been better for me to kill the guy?" Sheela said, subconsciously practicing a few dance steps to the musician's notes, "I mean, I just don't think them being guards for a jerk's business justifies them dying is all..."

"I'm not hearing this, okay?" Bellows said with some irritation, "Gerhard had the rest of us leave so we wouldn't be involved if you lot got caught, alright? I'll keep mum about it this time, but seriously girl, you have got to learn some discretion."

"Ah yes, 'discretion'," Sheela said, hiking her bosom up further and sticking one leg so far out that the only break in her shown skin was the belt keeping her skirt together on that side, "Because the only female goblin in the group, the one who dresses as provocatively as she can get away with, is somehow going to not to stick out."

"Right, why would I expect subtlety from you?" the musician said, laughing away the tension, "On that note, is Fen still giving you the cold shoulder?"

"Ugh, yes," the gobliness said, standing back up and straightening her garments, "I mean, I'm good on magic right now, so it doesn't really matter, but still. The only time I see him is when we all rehearse together, and even then he keeps his distance."

"Yeah, I've heard similar stuff from some of the other women," the dwarfess said, "I guess he's one of those guys that just wants you once, then doesn't want anything to do with you."

"That seems dumb," Sheela said, folding her arms.

"Taken a bit of a shine to him, then?" Bellows said, waggling her eyebrows.

"N-no," the little dancer said, "Not really. I'm just not used to a man not being interested in me is all." Her face and voice betrayed the fact that there was a bit of emotion tied to the situation, however.

"Well, take it from me, whatever you are or aren't feeling, it isn't worth your time," the musician said, gesturing up and down the gobliness' body, "You're a fine figure of a young woman, so I know you can do better than some tumbler. Heck, even if you just end up doing sex work like you want, you'll make a heck of a lot more money than if you let yourself get tied down."

"You're probably right," Sheela said with a little disdain in her voice, "I'm shouldn't let myself get wrapped up in things like this. Thanks, Bellows."

Her mind calmed after the conversation, the gobliness was able to dedicate more time back to her study of magic in the evenings. After practicing her new rune to the point that she could reproduce it at will, she considered inscribing it into her skin, but decided to wait. The sword she had gotten was the only thing she had that was sharp enough to cut the fine, specific lines needed, but would be far to unwieldy to do the minute work needed. Instead, she decided that, upon reaching the next town, she would find a healer or someone who supplies them, and get what she needed there. In the meantime, she empowered a few more paper runes, just in case.

Upon arrival, Briar Glen turned out to be more of a permanent camp than an actual town. Hundreds of carts, tents, and wagons were roughly circled up around a central point that Sheela could not immediately glimpse. The only indication that it existed somewhere in the mess were the two tall poles that seemed to reach up into the sky for no apparent reason. Unlike in Mirfield, the caravan seemed to scatter as they entered the town, with only a few wagons staying together. However, come the evening, even their occupants had mostly wandered off to other places. Lacking any real reason to wait for the still-dour Nora to return, the gobliness set out to find out what was going on.

At first, the camp seemed like any other night in the caravan, just with many more people and wagons. Happy chatter drifted up around roaring cooking fires, the sounds of music and laughter filled the air, and there were even a few places where debauched acts were happening in the open.

'Oooooo, Nora would be furious if she saw that,' Sheela thought with a grin, walking toward the scantily clad woman as she bowed and was replaced by a lithe-looking man in a similar state of undress.

"Hi there," she said, "My name's Sheela. What's yours?"

When the woman looked down at her in surprise, the little lady began to wonder if she had made a mistake.

"I'm sorry," the dancer said, "I...didn't know there were goblins here as well. I'm sure someone else can give you directions back to wherever you came from, though! So sorry."

Sheela opened her mouth to say something, but the woman was hurrying away before she had the chance to respond. As the gobliness tried to understand what had just occurred, she looked around, scanning the area for any clues. After a few seconds of thinking all was well, she finally realized that everyone within her sight was human. Furthermore, she realized that everyone she had encountered since leaving the wagon had been human as well.

Feeling suddenly very self-conscious and out of place, she started searching all over for some indication of where to go. Without any sense of direction, the little lady began to panic, but caught sight of the tall poles that she believed to be in the center of the traveller's town, and made as straight of a shot for them as she could.

People around the tents and wagons that surrounded her scoffed as she passed, and the wide lane the gobliness raced along became narrower as she moved toward the hub, giving her a sensation of being crushed. The sudden openness of the temporary town's "square" was no better, simply due to the volume of people inhabiting it. Sheela's run came to an immediate stop as the little lady became quickly entangled in the legs of the milling crowd. Though large numbers of people usually made her feel safer, the sheer number of bodies in the throng felt suffocating.

Music crashed and conflicted in the air above her, the sound of various bands playing without regard for one another's performances. The mass audience pressed in on them, applauding and jeering as they pleased, and in the process, Sheela was carried along by the movements of those larger than herself. In order to avoid being trampled, she took what openings she could find, and eventually found herself along the edge of the large wooden stage where the musicians played.

The platform was the only solidly built structure she had seen in the town thus far, with enough space to accommodate at least four separate theatrical performances at once. Signs for various acts were hung from the tall polls, and there were even pulleys attached to them for raising flags or scenery. The musicians, who each had a considerably smaller footprint than any theatre troupe, seemed to have their own audience each. For the most part, those crowds matched the races of the band they were listening to, and each had its own way of enjoying themselves.

Wherever human musicians played, their listeners were singing along with the somber, yet somehow lively, harmonies of their ballads, swaying reverently in time with the stories of their past. Elsewhere, Sheela could see and hear the upbeat rhythms of the dwarfs as they laughed and drank with the music. These groups were fewer, but possibly the loudest, as the small people's deep voices carried farther. A single, small orc crowd surrounded their own band, and was the only group that others gave a berth to, no doubt due to the spectators' rather aggressive dance style. The little lady's attention continued on quickly as, though the orc's harsh melody's were quite interesting, their heavy use of percussion reminded her uncomfortably of the music made by her fellow goblins.

Finally, as her head was swimming with the press of bodies and nauseating mixture of musical styles, the little spotted a familiar face. Within the audience of a nearby elfen group, Fenian listened, unaware of her presence. Though Sheela knew she would regret going to him, he was the only person she recognized in the chaotic scene, and therefore her only hope.

Angry voices yelled down at the small woman as she shoved past the people around her. Often, the easiest route was just to follow the edge of the stage, but the mass of people sometimes pressed so tightly against it that she had to push through what gaps she could find further back. In the back of her mind, she wondered if the children of larger races knew how lucky they were to eventually grow out of her height range.

Each group had its own distinct smells and sounds, and when the scent around her shifted from the sweaty, earthen odor of humanity to a naturally floral aroma, the gobliness began to move more carefully. She looked up into each face, hoping he had not already moved on.

"Fenian," Sheela said, crying out, "Fen, where are you?" Her voice, normally on the nasal side, cracked higher out of fear.

Displeased eyes were cast down upon the little lady, contributing further to her anxiety. Each time she thought she found the man, a clearer look at the face of the person made it clear they were not him. Murmurs began to spread through the crowd, their tones clearly scandalized, despite the pretty lilt of the Elfen tongue.

"Someone lost a child!"

"...no kid, that's a goblin..."

"...where did that filth came from?"

Her heart beating faster by the second, Sheela spun about, trying desperately to ignore the soft hail of loathing being passed around the crowd at her mere existence. She spotted one head moving away, its back to her, and decided to take a chance. Though many in the group had similarly blond hair, any movement that would take her from the throng of disproving eyes seemed like a good idea. As the knot of people loosened, however, the gobliness realized that she had done the opposite of escape.

The area she had moved into was far more ornately decorated than the human camp had been. Festooned in silks, filigree, and bright enamel paints, the area could not be mistaken for anything other than elfen, even by someone who had next to no exposure to their culture. Those people who noticed her either continued the whispers of the crowd or became amused by the disparity of her presence.

"Fenian!" Sheela said loudly. With more open sightlines, she had gotten a better look at the person who was moving away from her, and knew it was him. He began to move more quickly when he heard her voice.

"Please, wait!" she said, trying desperately to catch up with him. She stumbled several times, but did not fall completely. The little lady bunched the fabric of her skirt in one fist and continued her bull rush toward the only thing her frightened mind recognized.

"Go away," Fenian said angrily, "You can't be here!"

"I'm sorry," she said, gasping for breath as she continued to run after the furiously walking elf, "I'm really sorry, I know I shouldn't be talking to you, but-" She nearly slammed into the back of his legs, not having realized that the man had stopped.

"You're damn right, you shouldn't," he said, his voice a hiss, "What is your problem? I specifically told you my kind wouldn't welcome you!"

"I couldn't find anyone else I knew," Sheela said, choking back tears, "I just wanted to look around, but everyone was looking at me, and I panicked..."

"Of course they were looking at you," Fenian said, gesturing to her body, still clothed in her rather immodest dance costume, "you're dressed like a whore, you stupid koake!"

Though he had not struck her, the elf's words hit the gobliness like a firm slap in the face. Fear gave way to rage, and for a moment she shook uncontrollably, seemingly ready to unleash herself upon him.

"Really?" he said, "What are you going to do? Burn this place to the ground, too?"

A new sensation began in the back of Sheela's skull and began to creep across the rest of her body.

"You know why I'm angry," Sheela said quietly, "Why would you call me that, you...you..."

It felt like a stream of cold water was passing through her veins, turning all of her fury and sadness into pity. Her breathing slowed, and she unballed her fists. Despite the physical facts, the man before her was suddenly very small in her eyes.

"...you really don't care about anyone but yourself, do you?" she said, a touch of disbelief in her voice, "Everything you do is for your own pleasure. I cannot believe I let my feelings blind me to that."

"Everyone is only looking out for themselves, Sheela, even you," he said, "The sooner you learn that, the better off you'll be."

The crowd around them was beginning to gather closer. Looking around, the gobliness could tell that she was not welcome. Reaching into her brassiere, she extracted a rune, and looked at it for a few seconds. She could feel the power it held crackling in her fingers.

'I could just use this,' she thought, 'but then I wouldn't be any better than my father, would I?'

Casting her eyes back up to his, she tossed the scrap of paper at his feet.

"There's your trophy," she said, "I hope one day, someone hurts you are badly as you just hurt me."

With that, the little lady turned her back on the elfen acrobat, and walked away.

XIV

For the first time since she left the mines, Sheela really sauntered as she walked. Unlike the dance-step she had begun to use when happy, this walk gave off an air of superiority. She no longer cared if people were looking down upon her. Instead, she flaunted herself proudly, full of the knowledge that nobody had any power over her unless she allowed them to, and that she could instead even have power over them if she wanted.

Even in the other camps she passed through on the way back, the gobliness felt people's eyes upon her. She relished the sensation, and it fed her growing self-confidence. The town-sized camp was much larger than she had realized as she ran about it in her earlier state of distress, and it took the better part of the night to find her way back to Nora's wagon. By the time she finally made it there, however, the little lady knew exactly what she was going to do.

Stepping inside, she surveyed the small room which had once seemed so welcoming. In her mind, it was no longer a destination, but merely a stop on the way to wherever she was going in life.

"And where will I go?" she said quietly, while checking that her fabric and coins were still safe in the bag she had purchased. When she started to fill a waterskin, the noise finally awoke Nora.

"Mmmwhat are you doing, just getting back?" the sandy-haired gypsy said.

"I'm leaving," Sheela said, not looking at the other woman.

"What happened?" Nora said wearily, sitting up slowly.

"Why do you care?" the gobliness said, "You haven't spoken to me for nearly a week. Why now?"

"You're a talented dancer, if nothing else," the human woman said, the first real interest in her voice since before the trip to Thorne's, "I...would hate to lose a good performer."

"And yet, you don't want me to do what I'm best at," the little lady said.

"Well, dance is one thing, but-" the gypsy said.

"Enjoying sex is wrong?" Sheela said, giving her a look that was full of daggers, "Honestly, it's just so strange to me. I keep hearing hints that something bad happened to you, and I get that, I really do. But why let your past ruin something you enjoy?"

The shocked expression on the sandy-haired woman's face indicated that she was completely awake after the gobliness' outburst.

"It's not that enjoying sex is wrong…" Nora said, searching for her words, "But if you treat it so flagrantly, treat it like a thing to be sold, people won't respect you. They'll mistreat you..." She had a distant look in her eyes.

"I'm a goblin, Nora. People already don't respect me," Sheela said, a small laugh passing her lips before she continued, "I may as well respect myself enough to be able to make a living doing something I enjoy."

"It's not right, though," the gypsy said, her voice starting to waver.

"Who decided that?" the little lady said, her own voice taking on an edge, "Just because it isn't right for you doesn't mean it isn't for me."

"But the gods-" the human woman said.

"I don't know about your gods," the gobliness said, fed up, "but mine wanted me dead, remember? I've had enough of their kind. I'll get by on my own without some priest and his idol telling me what to do."

Locking eyes with Nora, and actually paying attention to them for the first time that evening, Sheela saw that the other woman's eyes held regret. For the smallest moment, she contemplated inquiring further about what had happened to the gypsy to bring her to this point. Without another word, though, the little lady picked up her belongings and walked out of the wagon.

The sky above was turning orange as the sun began its ascent somewhere over the horizon. As she walked, the gobliness saw people waking up to perform their mundane daily tasks. She recognized some of them as revelers from the previous evening.

'Even they have a look shame in their eyes,' Sheela thought, 'They perform for others' entertainment, yet feel bad for taking part in it themselves? Why would anyone let themselves feel bad for indulging in what they enjoy?'

Walking the road once more, the cool leather of the rucksack touching her mostly exposed back, the gobliness stood proud. Where once she had been naked and full of fear, she strode clothed in the knowledge that she was free. When a wagon pulled up, its driver gave her an inquisitive and beguiled look.

"Where're you headed to?" the mustachioed man said, "Perhaps I could give you a ride?" His voice dripped with salacious intent.

"Mirfield is good," Sheela said, a shark-toothed grin on her face, "I'm going to be a seamstress."

Made in the USA
Columbia, SC
03 May 2024

35241831R00098